"I came here to tell you that my son will be four on October 2."

Rebecca looked at Jeff. "I don't know if you have any interest in him at all, but I thought I owed it to you to tell you that you're a father," she admitted.

Jeff grabbed her arm, stopping her. "I have a son? You're telling me that all this time you've neglected to tell me I had a son?"

"Yes."

"And you think I might not care? Do you think I've changed that much, Rebecca? Do you not know me at all? Yes, I want to be part of my son's life!"

"I knew you five years ago, Jeff. I don't know you now. Your fiancée may not be prepared to be a stepmom, even if *you* want to be involved in Joey's life. You need to take that into consideration."

"Hell, I haven't had time to consider *anything*," Jeff said forcefully. At the moment his entire world was being turned upside down, and he had a lot of things to take into consideration—including his unresolved feelings for Rebecca.

Judy Christenberry

REBECCA'S LITTLE SECRET

HARLEQUIN®

TORONTO • NEW YORK • LONDON
AMSTERDAM • PARIS • SYDNEY • HAMBURG
STOCKHOLM • ATHENS • TOKYO • MILAN • MADRID
PRAGUE • WARSAW • BUDAPEST • AUCKLAND

ISBN 0-373-75037-4

REBECCA'S LITTLE SECRET

Copyright © 2004 by Judy Christenberry.

ABOUT THE AUTHOR

Judy Christenberry has been writing romances for over fifteen years because she loves happy endings as much as her readers do. A former French teacher, Judy now devotes herself to writing full-time. She hopes readers have as much fun with her stories as she does. She spends her spare time reading, watching her favorite sports teams and keeping track of her two daughters. Judy lives in Texas.

Books by Judy Christenberry

HARLEQUIN AMERICAN ROMANCE

*Brides for Brothers
†Tots for Texans
**Children of Texas

Don't miss any of our special offers. Write to us at the following address for information on our newest releases.

Harlequin Reader Service
U.S.: 3010 Walden Ave., P.O. Box 1325, Buffalo, NY 14269
Canadian: P.O. Box 609, Fort Erie, Ont. L2A 5X3

Chapter One

"Rebecca, I found a job for you!" Vivian Greenfield exclaimed as Rebecca Barlow entered the house. Her fall semester had begun this morning at the university, but she was looking for a part-time job to bring in some money to help pay her tuition.

"You have, Vivian? What kind of job?" Rebecca had worked at the nearby mall all summer selling clothes, and she was hoping for something with a more flexible schedule now that she was back in school again. She hadn't taken classes since her life had been turned upside down when she'd discovered she was pregnant almost five years ago.

"You would be working in the law office of Murphy and Jenkins. They've been my legal representatives for a long time, and Harriet, the office manager, said she could use some help."

Rebecca didn't much like lawyers, especially since her son's biological father was one, but Vivian made it impossible to do anything but thank her. "Is it a large firm?" Rebecca asked after hugging and thanking Vivian.

"Heavens, no. That's what I like about it. Harriet said you could come in tomorrow for your first day."

Rebecca went upstairs to her bedroom. She'd moved into Vivian's Dallas house in May, after Vivian's husband, Will, had found her and her son, Joey, and insisted they leave Arkansas with him.

Rebecca had been so happy to have family at last. She not only found her blood sister, Vanessa, but she gained Vanessa's mother and stepfather. They were such warm, loving people. They'd made a major difference in Joey's life. So Rebecca felt sure that she could handle any kind of job, if only to please Vivian.

The next afternoon, when Rebecca arrived at her new job, there were no lawyers in sight.

"It's vacation time," Harriet Graham reported. "Next week we'll be back hard at work. That gives you four days to learn as much as you possibly can."

Everything quickly fell into place for Rebecca. She went to classes every morning and worked with Harriet in the afternoons. Then she hurried to Vivian's home and spent her evenings with her beloved son. Joey would be four in October. He was already attending preschool and enjoying being with other children his age. He seemed happy and settled.... Unlike Rebecca's own childhood.

She and her siblings had been separated from one another. Some had been adopted, and some went into the foster-care system. Both Rebecca and her twin, Rachel, almost three years old at the time, had been adopted by different parents. Her brother David, five at the time, had been adopted by another family. Vivian and her first husband had adopted Vanessa, who was about three months old then. But Walter, seven, and James, eight, had been put in foster homes.

Will, Vivian's new husband, was the private investigator she'd hired to find Vanessa's siblings. Rebecca was the first they'd found. Vivian had taken her in as if she were a long-lost daughter. It was a welcome change in Rebecca's life after her adoptive parents had thrown her out when she discovered she was pregnant. She was thrilled to live in the house with Vivian, Will and Vanessa. She loved having a family to surround her son with.

Joey wasn't the only one to benefit from family. Rebecca did as well. She had talked to her adoptive mother a few times after Joey's birth, but the woman was too afraid of her husband to actually have a relationship with Rebecca. Having stood alone through her pregnancy and Joey's young life, it meant a lot to Rebecca to have family to rely on.

And the prospect of having even more family was just so exciting. Will was looking for her and Vanessa's siblings. He'd actually found James, but he was serving in the Middle East in his capacity as a marine. Rebecca's twin, Rachel, and their brother David had not yet been discovered. Their brother Walter, sadly, had lost his life in combat years ago.

So everything seemed to be moving along smoothly until Friday afternoon.

"Jeff just called. He and his fiancée will drop by this afternoon," Harriet announced with some pride.

"Who is Jeff?" Rebecca asked cautiously.

"He's our boss. Didn't I tell you?"

"Is he Murphy or Jenkins?" Rebecca held her breath, praying that Harriet would choose one of those two names.

"Neither one," Harriet said with a laugh. "Jeff was Mr. Jenkins's nephew, but his name is Jacobs. He worked with his uncle, Mr. Jenkins, for several years, until he died. Mr. Murphy died five years ago. Jeff's wonderful. You'll enjoy working for him."

Harriet was sorting through a file as she talked and didn't see Rebecca's face turn white. Rebecca abruptly sat down in a chair before she fell over. She couldn't believe it. Jeff Jacobs. She hadn't seen Jeff in five years, and now she'd ended up working for him? Impossible.

"His fiancée is very nice, too. You'll like her. She's the perfect wife for Jeff. She has great contacts in the area. She was a debutante, of course, and her family has lived here for four generations."

"How…nice." Jeff was engaged. Well, that explained a lot. She should've expected it. He was handsome, charming and now a lawyer. He was sure to be chased by women.

"Oh, here they come now. He must've called on his cell phone. I didn't expect them this soon," Harriet said, all smiles. Obviously she adored Jeff.

Rebecca had hoped she could make up an excuse and leave before Jeff came in, but it was too late.

Jeff Jacobs entered the office with a smile on his face, holding his fiancée's hand. He bent over and kissed Harriet's cheek. "Did you miss me, Harriet?"

"Never," Harriet said with a cheeky grin. "Hello, Chelsea. You look very nice."

Rebecca didn't move, hoping Harriet would forget about her. She couldn't take her eyes off Jeff. After all, it had been five years since she'd last seen him. He hadn't changed much. His shoulders had broadened a little. Maybe he had a few new laugh lines, but they didn't detract from his looks.

"Where's our newest employee?" Jeff asked.

Rebecca rose from the chair she'd fallen into that had partially blocked her from their view. She had to. She wasn't a child. She wouldn't run and hide.

"Oh, here she is. Rebecca Barlow, and she's a good worker." Harriet beamed at Rebecca, sharing her good will.

Rebecca looked at Jeff, saying nothing.

"Well, Rebecca Bar—Becca? Becca, is that you? Where did you come from? Where have you been?" He crossed the room and wrapped his arms around her for a tight embrace.

He held her closely against him. Rebecca couldn't have moved if she'd wanted to. But she didn't. She'd forgotten how wonderful it was to feel his arms around her. She wished this feeling would never end...even though she knew it was about to.

Jeff swayed back and forth. "I looked for you everywhere. I even went back to Arkansas to find you. You'd disappeared. I kept waiting for you to contact me. Where did you go? What happened between you and your parents?" he demanded, backing away but not letting go of her.

Before she could even begin to compose an answer, his fiancée, Chelsea, took charge. "Perhaps you should introduce me, Jeff?"

"Oh, yeah, sure. This is Rebecca…Barlow, was it? We were in school together in Arkansas. After I moved, I lost track of her. Though that wasn't her name at the time. You married?"

"No. I found out my real name from Mom. I was adopted."

"What? They weren't your real parents? That must've been a shock! How did you—" he began, but Chelsea interrupted.

"Jeff, I hate to rush you, but we did tell Mother we'd be there early for dinner."

"Yes, of course. Is there anything I need to deal with immediately, Harriet?" Jeff asked, but his gaze remained fixed on Rebecca.

"No, there's nothing urgent," Harriet assured him, frowning.

"Okay, I'll see you Monday. Rebecca, will you be here Monday afternoon? I'd like to hear more about what happened to you."

Rebecca said yes, but she wasn't sure about her returning to her newly found job. She had a major decision to make that would affect her life greatly.

Whether or not to tell Jeff Jacobs that he was the father to her almost-four-year-old Joey.

"MOMMY! DIDN'T YOU HEAR ME?"

"What, honey? Oh, I'm sorry, Joey. I had something on my mind. What did you ask?"

"Will you play ball with me? Grandpa Will showed me how to throw it."

The sun was shining outside, and Rebecca couldn't think of any reason not to grant her son's wish, so she nodded and followed an enthusiastic Joey outside. He had benefited from Will's masculine influence.

But he would benefit even more from his biological father's influence.

That thought had played in Rebecca's head all weekend. And she still hadn't made up her mind. If she told Jeff and he wanted to be a part of Joey's life, it might affect his engagement. Was it fair to do that to Jeff? But was it fair not to tell him about Joey at all?

"Mommy! You didn't catch it!"

Rebecca looked up to see the white ball rolling past her. "Oh, sorry, honey." She picked up the ball and rolled it back to Joey.

"You're supposed to throw it back. Grandpa Will said."

"But I'm afraid it might hit you. I think you need to grow more before I throw it to you."

"I'm big enough. Come on, Mommy."

Rebecca complied, gently tossing the ball to her son, holding her breath that he wouldn't get hurt. After half an hour, she told him it was his naptime.

"Mommy, I'm too old to take naps!" he complained.

"Well, it's quiet time, really. You can lie on your bed and read one of your books, if you want."

"Can I watch television?" he pleaded.

"No. I want you to read." Not that he really could read, but he knew most of his books by memory. He could look at the pictures and remember the story.

He wasn't happy with her decision, but she didn't mind. Being a parent meant you had to disappoint your child every once in a while.

What if Jeff didn't know anything about parenting? What if he gave in to every demand Joey made? That would undo everything she had already set up with Joey and that would be terrible. Maybe that was another reason not to tell him.

Rebecca was going crazy trying to make the decision. In her heart of hearts, she knew she should tell Jeff the truth. But this was a life-altering decision, one that couldn't be taken lightly. For whatever she decided, it would affect not only her and Jeff, but most important, Joey. She just wanted to do right by him.

After she got Joey settled in his room, she knocked on the door of Vanessa's room. Having a sister to discuss things with was one of the newfound joys of family life.

"Rebecca, come on in," Vanessa said, swinging open her door.

"I need someone to talk to," Rebecca said apologetically.

"Sit down," Vanessa said, waving her sister to the only chair in the room while she sprawled on her bed. "Is something wrong?"

"Sort of. You know your mom found me a job at that law firm?"

"Yes. Isn't it going well?"

"It was going well until today. The only lawyer in the office came back from vacation today."

"Is he awful? Did he make a pass at you?"

"No, not that. Vanessa, he's—he's Joey's father."

Vanessa stared at her. "How can that be? You got pregnant in Arkansas and had Joey there, didn't you?"

"Yes. But Joey's father was a prelaw student then. He left because his parents died and he moved in with his aunt and uncle here in Dallas."

"Oh, my. What are you going to do?"

"I don't know. I've been trying to decide if I should tell him about Joey."

"He doesn't know? Well, of course you should tell him. He has a right to know."

"Are you sure? He's engaged to another woman. What if she doesn't want a stepson and it breaks up his engagement? Would that be fair?"

"Hmm. I think you should talk to Mom and Will about it. They're wiser than I am."

"Will they mind?"

"Of course not. Mom will be pleased. Come on. I think they're in the library. Will was going to do some paperwork while Mom read a book."

When the two young ladies entered the library, they discovered Will working at the desk, but Vivian was dozing in a big chair.

Will greeted them quietly. "Do you need something?"

Vanessa stepped closer. "Rebecca has a pretty big

problem and wanted to ask you and Mom what you think she should do, but Mom's asleep and—"

"I am not," Vivian protested, having awakened while Vanessa talked. "What's the problem?"

"Are you sure you don't mind?" Rebecca asked hesitantly.

"Of course not, child. I don't know why I fell asleep. I just seem to be tired lately."

Will smiled at his wife. "I think maybe you need a checkup, Vivian. You may be low in iron or something."

She made a face at him but promised to make an appointment next week. "Now, what's the problem? Do you not like one of your classes?"

"No. I—I've found Joey's father."

Will looked at her sharply. After all, it was his business to find people who were lost. "I could've helped you if I'd known you were looking."

"I—I wasn't looking. It turns out he's the lawyer I'm working for."

Vivian stared at her. "Jeff Jacobs is Joey's father? Well, I would've thought better of him!"

"It's not his fault, Vivian. I never told him. I know I should have, but he left just before I found out I was pregnant. His aunt and uncle took him back to Texas. They weren't very friendly, kind of looking down their noses at me. Then when Mom and Dad threw me out, I decided it was just me and my baby on our own. I didn't make any attempt to find Jeff."

"I see. It must've been a big shock."

"Yes. And to add to the dilemma he's engaged." Rebecca didn't say anything else.

"Yes, I'd heard that. Chelsea Wexham, isn't it? Her family has been here for many years."

"Yes. My problem is, I know I need to tell Jeff about Joey. But what if I do and it breaks up his engagement?" Rebecca couldn't confess that she secretly hoped it would and that's why she couldn't make the decision. She didn't trust herself enough to do the right thing.

Will frowned. "I don't think you can let that stop you, Rebecca. I think Jeff deserves to know he's a father. You understand that he may not choose to be involved in Joey's life? I think that would be a bad decision, but he may choose it. Of course, you could sue for child support then."

"No! I wouldn't do that. But I feel guilty for not having told him before now."

"Will's right, dear. Better late than never. I'm sure he'll understand when you explain."

Rebecca wasn't sure Jeff would understand. She felt sure he would acknowledge Joey as his son, but he might never speak to her again.

"Are you sure?" she asked faintly, giving them one last chance to tell her she should run away and hide. Joey had been her only family for so long. She was a little worried about sharing him, even with Jeff. Jeff and his wife.

"If you want to do the right thing, Rebecca," Will said slowly, "then, yes, you have to tell Jeff about Joey."

"I know. I just dread facing him."

"I'll go with you when you tell him if you want me to," Will offered.

Rebecca actually smiled at his gesture. "Thank you, Will, but I think I'd better face the music alone. Though I guess I'll be looking for a new job after Monday."

"We'll help you find one, dear," Vivian assured her. "There has to be another job available."

All Rebecca could do was smile gratefully. Already she was struggling with how she would face Jeff and tell him about his son.

JEFF JACOBS WAS DISTRACTED all weekend long. He tried to hide it, but he felt sure Chelsea realized it. And the reason for his distraction. He'd tried to explain the surprise of seeing Rebecca there in his own office after having looked for her five years ago. But he hadn't succeeded.

He needed time to absorb Rebecca's return to his life. And he needed the answers to a lot of questions. Like why had her parents kicked her out of their house. Her father had been difficult, but he hadn't threatened to disown her before. But when Jeff had called the house, her father had told him she didn't live there anymore. Then he'd hung up.

Jeff had called back the next day when he knew her mother would be the only one at home. She had said the same thing, only in a nicer tone of voice. But she'd added that she couldn't say anything else.

He'd flown up the next weekend and visited their

old haunts. He'd already discovered that Rebecca was no longer attending classes at university. He checked with Information, too, but she wasn't listed. He even went so far as to check with the police.

He'd come back to Dallas distraught. His uncle had just lost his wife to cancer, after their trip to Arkansas. That was the reason Jeff hadn't managed to call Rebecca right away. He'd done what he could for his aunt and uncle. After all, they had taken him in and raised him.

So he and his uncle mourned together. After a year or so, his uncle began to push him to date. Jeff did so, because he understood his uncle's reasoning. He met several nice women, but still, he kept Rebecca in his heart. Gradually his memories dulled.

After a while, he began to think about his future. After his uncle's death, he realized how important family was. When he met Chelsea, he didn't "fall in love" with her, as he had with Rebecca, but she was a nice woman and they became friends.

When she pushed for something more than friendship, he agreed and proposed marriage. Now he wondered why he'd done such a thing.

When he got to work Monday morning, he questioned Harriet about Rebecca.

"I only know she's Vivian's daughter's sister. And she's living with them. She's a lovely girl."

"Yes, she is. When does she come in to work?"

"At one, after her classes."

"Fine, I want to talk to her when she comes in."

"Yes, sir." Harriet didn't make any comment, but

Jeff avoided her knowing gaze and escaped to his office. He didn't need anyone to remind him about Chelsea.

He settled into his office, trying to concentrate on business while he waited to see Rebecca again.

AFTER REBECCA'S LAST CLASS, she darted into the ladies' room and combed her hair and powdered her nose. It was going to be hard enough to face Jeff without knowing her nose was shining. When she'd done all she could to improve her appearance, she reluctantly gathered her books and walked the two blocks to her job.

As she entered the office, she immediately said to Harriet, "I need to speak to Jeff as soon as I can."

"Really? Well, he wants to talk to you, too. Just a minute." She picked up the phone and said, "Jeff, Rebecca is here and would like to meet with you as soon as possible."

After she hung up the phone, she said, "Go right in, Rebecca."

Rebecca had expected questions from Harriet, and she hadn't been sure how she would answer them. But there were no questions. Oh, well, she would face questions when she talked to Jeff.

He stood and came across the room to greet her. "Come in, Becca." He reached for her, as if he were about to hug her again.

Rebecca drew back. She couldn't bear such close contact with what she had to tell him. "I—I need to talk to you."

Jeff frowned. "Of course, I want to talk to you, too."

Without waiting to be asked, Rebecca sat down in one of the big leather chairs in front of his desk. She didn't think her legs would continue to hold her up.

To her surprise, Jeff sat down in the other chair, close to her. "Aren't—aren't you going to sit in your chair behind the desk?"

He laughed. "This isn't a legal matter, is it? We're just friends talking, aren't we?"

Rebecca didn't smile. And she couldn't answer his question. Looking away from him, she said, "Look, Jeff. I'm sure you have many questions for me, but I need to tell you the truth about why my parents disowned me."

"Okay, but whatever it was that you did, I doubt that I'll agree with their decision. That's not how parents should behave."

"It's not something *I* did," she protested indignantly. "It's something *we* did."

He stared at her.

Without waiting for him to ask a question, she stumbled on, hoping their conversation would soon be over. "After you left, I discovered I was pregnant."

Jeff continued to stare at her, horror dawning in his eyes. "That's why your parents—damn! I'm sorry. I should have been there for you. I guess you had no choice about what to do. Why didn't you call me?"

"Because it was obvious your aunt and uncle considered me unsuitable. If my own parents thought me white trash, I figured your relatives would, too.''

''Surely you didn't think I would think you below me?''

''I don't know. I was in shock. I had a little savings, and my mother slipped me some money. It was difficult at first.''

He reached over to take her hand, but she wouldn't let him touch her.

''I'm sorry, Becca. I wish I'd known and we wouldn't have lost our baby.''

She stared at him. ''You think I had an abortion? You think I killed our baby?'' Her voice rose in horror.

''I understand. You were all alone. You didn't have many options.''

''I came to tell you that my son will be four on October 2. I don't know if you have any interest in him at all, only learning about him now. That's fine. I thought I owed it to you to tell you that you are a father.'' She got up out of her chair and headed for the door.

He grabbed her arm, stopping her. ''I have a son? You're telling me you had the baby and all this time you neglected to tell me that I had a son?''

Chapter Two

"Yes," Rebecca said succinctly, a mixture of guilt and irritation affecting her.

"And you think I might not care? Do you think I've changed that much, Rebecca? Do you not know me at all? Do you think I don't miss having family, someone of my own blood? Yes, I want a part in my son's life.

"In fact, I think you owe me the next four years, since you managed to take the first four years without me."

"Have you finished ranting?" she asked coldly.

"No, I haven't!" he snapped back. "I have four years' worth of ranting stored up. How dare you not tell me that I had a child! You know me better than to think I wouldn't care!"

"I knew you five years ago, Jeff. I don't know you at all now. Your fiancée may not be prepared to be a stepmom, even if you want to be involved in Joey's life. You need to take that into consideration."

"Hell! I haven't had time to consider anything. And that's your fault!" He was almost shouting now.

The office door opened. "Jeff, is everything all right?" Harriet asked hesitantly.

"No, Harriet, it's not. Come in here."

"Jeff, I don't think—" Rebecca began.

"Do you think I'm going to keep my son a secret, Rebecca? That I'm ashamed of him? Well, I'm not. And I'm going to be involved in his life, so Harriet might as well know."

"And do you need to yell when you tell Harriet?" Rebecca asked, her features cold.

"I can yell if I want to. It's my office!"

"Jeff, I've never seen you like this. What's wrong?" Harriet demanded, giving him a motherly look.

"Rebecca gave birth to my son nearly four years ago and she's just getting around to telling me."

Harriet looked shocked.

Rebecca wanted to walk out of the office and never see either of them again. Jeff wasn't even trying to understand. Okay, he had a right to be angry, but he was throwing a temper tantrum in Rebecca's opinion.

"And she gave him up for adoption?" Harriet asked, obviously following her own line of thought.

"No, she didn't do that."

Harriet turned to Rebecca. "You kept your baby and raised him by yourself? That must've been hard."

Unwanted tears filled Rebecca's eyes at Harriet's sympathy. She quickly looked down so no one would see such weakness. "Yes, it was, Harriet. Thank you for saying that."

"Is the boy here in Dallas with you now? Vivian

didn't mention him to me. Does he look like Jeff?''
Harriet moved closer to Rebecca.

"I'm not sure. Do you want to see a picture of
him?'' Rebecca only made the offer to Harriet, but
when she opened her billfold to show Harriet, Jeff
came to look, too.

"Look, Jeff. He looks just like you. What a fine
boy!'' Harriet turned to Rebecca. ''You've done a
good job raising him.''

"I hope so. I've tried.''

Jeff turned his back to both women and rubbed his
neck. Then he turned around. ''Becca, I owe you an
apology for my reaction. I'm still angry that I've been
robbed of the first four years of my son's life, but I'm
grateful to you for giving him life and for taking good
care of him.''

"And I apologize for not contacting you. But you
hadn't called and I thought you'd move on to a—a
better life. I convinced myself you wouldn't be interested. I developed a mentality of me and Joey against
the world.''

"His name is Joey?'' Jeff asked urgently.

She nodded.

"My dad's name was Joe.''

"I know.''

"You named him after my dad?'' Jeff asked, his
eyes filling with tears.

"His full name is Joseph Lee Barlow.''

Jeff had been named Jefferson Lee by his father.
Rebecca wanted Joey to have some part of his father

in his name. Jeff turned away again. After he composed himself, he said, "I want to see him."

Harriet said, "You don't have anything on your schedule except for Mrs. Yancy wanting to change her will again. I can reschedule her."

"Thanks, Harriet. Ready, Rebecca?"

Rebecca felt like she'd lost track of what was happening. "Ready for what?"

"I want to see Joey. Now. Will you introduce me to my son?"

"Yes, but—but I haven't told him. I haven't prepared him—"

"Good. Let's go."

"IF YOU'LL WAIT HERE," Rebecca said, having led Jeff to the library, "I'll go find Joey."

"You don't know exactly where he is?"

"No. Betty will know." She left him alone and headed for the kitchen. "Betty, where's Joey?"

"What are you doing home now? Are you sick?" the housekeeper asked, moving toward her to touch her forehead.

"No, I'm not sick. I've brought Joey's daddy home to meet him."

Betty's eyes widened, but she didn't ask any questions. "Joey is helping Peter wash Miz Vivian's car."

"Thank you."

"Peter said he wouldn't let him get wet," Betty called after her as Rebecca headed for the driveway, where Peter, Betty's husband, was washing a car.

"Mommy!" Joey squealed in excitement. "I'm helping Peter!"

"I can see that, but I need you to come inside and meet someone."

Her son pouted and protested that Peter needed him, but Peter assured him there would be other car washes he could help with.

A disgruntled Joey followed his mother into the house. Once they were inside, Rebecca stopped. "Did you get wet?"

"Not much," Joey said, looking at his mother from under his lashes.

"I think we'd better go change. Joey," she said in what she hoped was a casual voice, "do you remember asking about your daddy?"

That question got Joey's attention. "Yeah. Why?"

"Because he's here. He didn't know about you until today, and he's come at once to meet you."

"My real daddy?" the little boy asked skeptically.

"Of course your real daddy. I wouldn't lie about that."

Her intention of changing Joey's clothes so he would impress his father went down the drain. Suddenly Joey darted toward the library. "Is he in here?" he asked over his shoulder.

"Yes, but—"

Joey was already through the door.

Rebecca hurriedly followed him in time to hear him say, "You're not my real daddy!"

"Joey, don't be rude, please. Let me introduce you to Jeff Jacobs. Jeff, this is Joey." She tightened her hands on her son's shoulders before she added, "And, yes, Jeff is your real daddy."

"But you told me he was strong like Superman! He doesn't even have a cape!"

Much to Rebecca's relief, Jeff laughed. "I'm a lot stronger than your mom. Maybe that's why she said that."

"Yeah. We was scared and she said if you was there, you'd protect us."

"We *were* scared, Joey," Rebecca corrected.

Joey gave her one of his disgusted looks. He didn't count grammar among the important things in life.

Jeff had been standing. Before the awkward silence got too long, he said, "May we sit down and talk a little? I've missed four years of your life. I'd like to know what you like to do. Your favorite foods, those kinds of things."

Joey looked at Jeff and then his mother.

Rebecca braced herself for what was coming.

"When we have something to celebrate, Mommy takes me to McDonald's!"

"Joey, you just had lunch. And it's not nice to ask to be invited." Rebecca felt her cheeks turning red.

"But, Mommy, he asked what I like. And I like to go there."

"Fair enough," Jeff said. "How about I take you there for dinner this evening?"

"That would be great. Me and Mommy will like that."

Rebecca hurriedly said, "I won't be going, honey. It's a chance for you to get to know your daddy."

Joey looked at Jeff and frowned. "I don't want to go without you, Mommy."

Before she could begin to persuade him, Jeff said, "That's fine if Mommy comes. I'll invite my fiancée, too, so you can meet her."

"What's a fiancée?" Joey asked.

"She's the lady I'm going to marry."

Joey backed up to lean against his mother's legs. "Uh-uh, I'm not changing mommies. I'm keeping my mommy."

Rebecca bent down and kissed her son's cheek. "I'm glad you want to keep me, sweetie, but that's not what your daddy meant. Chelsea would be your stepmother and I would be your mommy."

"Stepmother? Like the one in Cinderella? That would be bad! I don't want a stepmother!"

"Joey, mind your manners. I'll explain later."

Jeff looked at the little boy with his stubborn chin. "Maybe that's a good idea. You'll have time to explain everything and we can talk at McDonald's. Okay, squirt?"

"What's a squirt?" Joey asked.

"Your mom will explain that, too." Jeff moved toward the door. "About seven?"

"Actually," Rebecca said, "little boys like to eat around six, if you don't mind."

"I don't mind. You don't need to go back to work today. I'll explain to Harriet that you've got today off and that you'll be there tomorrow."

Rebecca froze. "You're not going to fire me?"

"Why would I do that?"

"Maybe because you're mad at me?"

"I'm not. Besides, my new partner comes in the morning. You'll be able to help out until he hires a full-time secretary."

JEFF SAT IN HIS CAR for several minutes, trying to take in all he'd learned this afternoon. He had a son. He'd always wanted children some day but this wasn't exactly how he'd expected to form his family. Still, he wanted to hold him, to hug him, to be there for him. But Jeff knew he was a stranger to Joey, and it would take him time to warm up to him and show his love.

He remembered the photo Rebecca pulled out. Joey looked like he did as a boy, but he did have Rebecca's stubborn chin. Jeff laughed. That was no surprise, but it probably explained how she managed to raise Joey alone.

Now he had to face Chelsea and explain how his life had changed in one afternoon. He was supposed to take her to dinner, and McDonald's wasn't what she would be expecting.

When he reached the Wexham home, he paused. Suddenly he realized that he didn't like the Wexhams' home. It wasn't a home. It was a house with expensive things in it. He couldn't see bringing Joey there.

Then he thought about Vivian Greenfield's house. Jeff had always liked her house. He'd first visited it almost five years ago with his uncle. Vivian's house was a home, warm and inviting. He wanted that kind of house for his son.

With a sigh, he got out of the car and went to the

door, ringing the doorbell. The housekeeper answered the door. She wasn't part of the family, like Betty and Peter. Mrs. Wexham never let her forget her place.

"Is Chelsea in?" he asked.

"Yes, sir. I'll tell her you're here." She led him to the parlor and left the room. He stood there, looking at the brocade antique sofa and the accompanying chairs. He decided that he would ask Chelsea to go for a ride. He certainly didn't want their conversation interrupted.

"Jeff! This is a surprise. How nice," Chelsea said with a beautiful smile.

"I know. I should've called but, well—you'll understand when I tell you what's happened. Can we go for a ride?"

She was wearing slacks and a shirt. "I'm not dressed to go out, Jeff. I could change—"

"No, Chelsea, we won't get out of the car. But this is important. Please."

She gave him a curious look. "All right. Let me tell Mother."

She came back several minutes later. "Sorry. She had to lecture me about going out like this," she said with a smile.

For the first time, Jeff considered what kind of parent Chelsea would be. He could picture Joey in a proper suit, standing rigidly at attention. And being seriously unhappy.

He shoved that thought away and led Chelsea to his BMW. He drove to a nearby park, pulled into a free space, then rolled down the windows and turned off the motor. It was a mild fall day, not too hot as long as there was a breeze.

"Okay, what happened today? Is it good? Did you get a new client?" Chelsea asked.

"It's more personal than that. It's rather complicated as well. Rebecca—Rebecca told me that she was pregnant when I left Arkansas. She has been raising my son alone since his birth."

"And she didn't tell you? Well, I think you've got a good case to get out of paying child support." Chelsea was looking at her nails, as if trying to decide if she liked the color.

"I have no intention of avoiding child support payments. He's my son."

"Are you sure? I think you should have a paternity test done. She could've gotten knocked up by some jerk who ran off and she sees an opportunity to get some money."

"Chelsea, how could you be so cold? Rebecca's not like that!" Jeff snapped.

"Jeff, you haven't seen her in five years. She may have changed." She looked up at him. "Right?"

"It's possible, I guess."

"So get the test."

"When you meet him, you'll understand why that isn't necessary."

She gave him a droll look. "We'll see."

"Yes, you will. Tonight. I invited Joey and Rebecca to join us for dinner tonight."

Before he could continue, Chelsea protested. "Jeff, I'm not sure that a five-star French restaurant allows children. And even if they do, a little boy won't like it.''

"I know. So we're going to McDonald's."

"You must be kidding. No one goes to McDonald's."

"People with children go to McDonald's. And I now have a child. I'm trying to be as honest as I can be, Chelsea. Joey is going to be a part of my life. I want him to be a part of your life, too."

"A little boy? How old is he?"

"He's almost four. He's in preschool."

"So we're talking visitation for an occasional weekend?"

Jeff sank his teeth into his bottom lip. "Maybe more than that. I'm not sure right now. Let's just take it one step at a time. We'll go to McDonald's and—"

"I don't want to go to McDonald's. I'll eat at home." She crossed her arms over her chest and stared at him.

"It's your choice. But Rebecca is coming with us, and you know how the gossips are." He shrugged his shoulders. "If you're with me, nobody will think anything of it."

He let his words settle into her head. Then he said, "But it's up to you, Chelsea. I don't want to force you to do something you don't want to do."

She glared at him. "I'll go, but you're going to owe me big time, Jeff Jacobs."

They drove to Chelsea's home in silence. It was wrong to compare Rebecca and Chelsea. They were two completely different people. And Rebecca had had time to get used to having a child. He couldn't imagine Chelsea pregnant or even having children, now that he thought about it. In fact, he couldn't believe the subject never came up before. And he needed to change that. Just before she got out of the car, he asked, "How many children do you want us to have?"

"I haven't really thought about it. But certainly none anytime soon. I want us to travel and to have fun together, just the two of us. Maybe we could have one child when I'm in my mid-thirties. That's still safe. But I don't think I'd want more than one."

She leaned over and kissed him before she got out of the car and went into the house.

Jeff couldn't believe how many momentous revelations had been brought to his attention today. How could he have proposed to Chelsea without ever asking her about children? He wanted children. More than one child. He'd been an only child and he'd hated it. It was lonely, and there was too much responsibility and burden to carry for one person, so much pressure and nobody to share it with.

Chelsea was one of two children. It had occurred to Jeff that her brother had been an accident, since there were seven years between them. But he hadn't asked. Maybe he didn't want to know…or maybe he was afraid of Chelsea's response.

REBECCA HAD SPENT THE afternoon talking to Joey about stepmothers and the advantage of having a father. By dinnertime, she'd made some progress, but not much.

Rebecca dressed in jeans and a cotton sweater, along with athletic shoes, then made sure her son was in clean clothes. She'd combed his hair, but it didn't behave very well. To her he looked adorable. She hoped Chelsea would think so.

She'd called Jeff and told him they would meet him at the fast-food restaurant since he had to pick up Chelsea. He reluctantly agreed. Rebecca and Joey arrived five minutes early. She ordered and paid for their food, so there would be no awkward confrontation later. They found a table for four and settled in on one side of the table. Joey wanted to open his meal at once, but Rebecca insisted he wait for the others to arrive and order their food.

When Jeff and Chelsea came in, Rebecca waved to them. Either she was severely underdressed or Chelsea was overdressed with her pink sleeveless top that didn't quite reach her waist and a skirt that flared around her thighs. Rebecca guessed that the top was made of cashmere, which made it very expensive, and out of place for this type of restaurant.

Jeff frowned when he saw they already had their food. Chelsea sat down at the table, and he asked her what she wanted. She asked for the kids' meal.

"Goody!" Joey exclaimed. "Can I have your toy if you don't want it?"

"Chelsea, I should introduce you to Joey, my son, who has already asked for your toy. If you want to keep it, please do so.'' Rebecca gave her son a re-proving look.

''Mommy! She wouldn't want a toy soldier!''

''She might, Joey, and I've told you it's not nice to ask for something.''

Joey ducked his head and muttered, ''Okay.''

Jeff promised to be right back and went to purchase their food. Rebecca tried to make conversation with Chelsea, but it was forced and awkward. They were all relieved when Jeff returned.

''Here's your meal,'' he told Chelsea as he sat the box in front of her. He had gotten a cheeseburger and fries for himself.

Rebecca told Joey he finally could open his box and begin eating.

He opened his box, but his interest was fixed on what toy he'd received. ''Oh. I got the green soldier.'' Disappointment filled his voice.

''What's wrong with the green soldier?'' Jeff asked.

''I already have three green soldiers, but I wanted a blue soldier.''

Chelsea looked up after opening her box. ''I have a blue soldier.'' Her voice was offhand.

Joey looked at his mother, but she shook her head no.

After a minute, when Chelsea had begun eating her hamburger, Joey said politely, ''I'll trade soldiers with you, if you want.''

Chelsea looked at Jeff, who nodded yes. She still hesitated a minute. Then she said, ''You can have it.''

Joey was thrilled. "Thank you!" he exclaimed.

Joey immediately began playing with the two soldiers. Rebecca had to remind him to eat his dinner, and the boy reluctantly took a bite of his hamburger. Jeff began asking him questions about what he liked to do, which also kept Joey busy.

Rebecca continued to try to make conversation with Chelsea while they ate, since she showed no interest in Jeff's conversation with Joey. "Did you attend Southern Methodist University?" Rebecca asked.

"No. I went to Stanford," Chelsea said, naming a highly ranked college in California.

"Oh. I've heard it's hard to get into Stanford."

"Not when my father went there *and* has contributed a lot of money to their building funds."

"How nice," Rebecca said. She couldn't think of any other comment.

"I majored in French Literature," Chelsea added.

"What kind of job can you get with that major?" Rebecca asked, truly curious about the practical application of her major.

Chelsea, however, appeared affronted. "A job? You think I'll be looking for a job? I'm marrying Jeff."

"Oh, of course," Rebecca agreed.

"Mommy! Look, there's Derek!" Joey squealed, jumping to his feet in his chair and knocking over his soda, splashing it all over Chelsea.

Chapter Three

"Oh, Joey, no!" Rebecca said, but it was too late to undo what Joey's excitement had done. "I'm so sorry, Chelsea," she hurriedly said, and began handing her all the napkins she had. "Joey, you need to apologize to Chelsea."

"I'm sorry. Mommy, can I go play with Derek?"

"No. Go get some more napkins for Chelsea," Rebecca ordered.

"More napkins won't help!" Chelsea snapped. "Look what he's done! My outfit is ruined and this is the first time I've worn it!"

"I'll pay to have it cleaned, Chelsea. Perhaps the cleaners can repair the damage," Rebecca said, hoping to satisfy Chelsea.

"I'm not sure they can do any good."

Joey returned with more napkins. "Here, Chelsea. I'm sorry I spilled my drink," Joey said, showing true contrition.

"You need to be more careful," she said, standing and backing away from him.

Jeff spoke for the first time. "I'd better take Chelsea home."

Rebecca nodded, biting her bottom lip to keep herself from responding to Chelsea's lack of understanding, and noting that Jeff didn't really stand up for his son or acknowledge that it was an accident.

Jeff rubbed Joey's hair and said, "I'll see you soon, Joey, okay?"

Joey nodded, but his gaze went to his mother, as if he wasn't sure that was a good idea.

Rebecca could understand her son's hesitation if seeing Jeff again meant seeing Chelsea. But she knew the woman wasn't used to being around children. She smiled encouragement to Joey. To Jeff, she said, "We're sorry. Please let me know how much the dry cleaning costs. We'll be glad to pay for it."

Jeff nodded and smiled, but Chelsea was standing by the door, her toe tapping out the seconds he kept her waiting. After Jeff reached her and held open the door, both Rebecca and Joey gave a sigh of relief.

"Now can I go play with Derek?"

"First you have to eat your hamburger. I'll get you some water to drink."

"But I want another soda."

"I think we'll stick with water."

His face took on a stubborn look. "I want a soda."

"You're not going to get a soda. If you're nice, you can play with Derek. If not, we'll just go home." Rebecca kept her voice calm, leaving the choice up to him.

"I'd like some water, please, Mommy." Joey even

managed to smile, determined he was going to play with his friend.

"Very nice. I'll be right back."

She brought him water, and he finished his hamburger in rapid fashion. Then he politely asked if he could go play with his friend.

Rebecca agreed, warning him they would have to leave in twenty minutes. After he ran to join his friend, she wished Jeff had been there to see his good behavior. And Chelsea, too. If she was going to be his stepmother, Rebecca wanted her to know that he could behave properly. He'd just gotten excited about seeing his friend.

REBECCA WASN'T EAGER TO GO to her job the next day. She was afraid Jeff would make remarks about Joey's behavior. It was important for Jeff to like Joey. Joey's self-image was at stake. She admitted to herself that his acceptance of Joey mattered to her, too. She wanted Jeff to believe she'd done a good job of raising their son.

Which also forced her to admit that Jeff's opinion about everything mattered to her, even if he was marrying another woman. All these years, even though she hadn't told Jeff about his son, she'd held him in her heart. She might not be able to have Jeff for her own, but she at least wanted her son to have him in his life.

She warily entered the law office that afternoon. When she barely avoided running into a tall, handsome man—not Jeff—she abruptly forgot her problems. "Oh, excuse me!" she exclaimed.

"I'm sure it was my fault. I was in too much of a hurry."

She smiled and stepped back, assuming he was on his way out of the office.

"Are you here about a legal problem?" he asked, not moving.

"No," Rebecca said, still smiling, "I work here."

"So do I." He gave her a curious look.

"Oh, you must be Jeff's new partner!" Rebecca exclaimed just as Harriet came out of Jeff's office.

"Oh, good, I see you two have met," Harriet said with a smile.

"Well, not exactly," the man said. "She's figured out I'm Jeff's new partner, but neither of us knows the other's name."

"Well, then, let me introduce you. Rebecca, this is Bill Wallace, Jeff's new partner, as you suspected. Bill, this is Rebecca Barlow, our part-time help."

"Hello, Rebecca," Bill immediately said. He extended his hand, and Rebecca placed hers in it, assuming he wanted to shake hands.

Bill, however, just held her hand, smiling at her. "I must say Jeff has shown great taste in hiring you."

Embarrassed, Rebecca tugged on her hand. "Actually, Harriet hired me."

"Then Harriet has shown good taste," he said, a teasing smile on his face as he continued to hold on to her hand.

Jeff walked out of his office. "What's going on?"

"I'm just making Rebecca's acquaintance," Bill assured him, his smile growing.

Jeff frowned. "I need to see you in my office, Bill."

Slowly Bill released Rebecca's hand. "I'll see you later, Rebecca," he promised before he turned and followed Jeff into his office.

"Close the door," Jeff snapped.

Bill did so, but his expression showed concern. "What's wrong? Did I commit a faux pas?"

"I just wanted to warn you about flirting with Rebecca." Jeff sat down behind his desk. "I don't think it's a good idea to mix business and personal interests."

"So she means nothing to you? Personally, I mean."

Jeff glared at him. "She's the mother of my son."

"Your son? I didn't know you had a son." Bill stared at him.

"I didn't know, either, until yesterday," Jeff admitted. "Rebecca and I had a—a relationship five years ago. I left rather suddenly and moved to Texas to be with my aunt and uncle. Because my aunt was dying of cancer, I didn't call Rebecca as soon as I'd wanted. By the time I tried to get hold of her, I couldn't find her."

"And she didn't contact you at all?"

"No."

"Must've been a real shock. How did Chelsea take it?"

"As well as could be expected. It will take Chelsea

time to adjust to the change." He wasn't sure Bill would believe him since he'd met Chelsea several times when they were talking about being partners.

"Yeah, I can imagine. Chelsea's used to getting her own way. You've spoiled her rotten."

"*I* have? Her family has certainly spoiled her, but I don't think I'm guilty of it," Jeff unhappily asserted.

"Well, Chelsea is the kind of lady you have to take a hard line with, to counterbalance her behavior."

"When I want your advice on how to handle my fiancée, I'll ask for it, Bill. Until then, mind your own business and keep away from Rebecca."

"Wait a minute! You've got Chelsea. Where does Rebecca fit in?"

"I told you. She's the mother of my son."

"So she has to take a vow of chastity?"

"I don't think she'd be interested right now."

"But if she indicates that she is, then there's no reason I can't get to know her better?"

"I told you I don't like mixing our personal lives with our business." Jeff frowned at his partner to emphasize his point.

"Jeff, she's a part-time worker, not another lawyer, or even my secretary. I'll be careful." With a triumphant smile, he left the office.

Jeff sat there, staring at a painting on the wall without even seeing it. He hated to admit it, but Bill was right. He didn't have the right to warn Bill away from Rebecca. Not when he was engaged to Chelsea.

And he was committed to Chelsea, of course. But when faced with Rebecca, living and breathing right there in front of him when he'd thought she was gone from him forever, he was growing more and more confused by the minute. He wasn't sure what he was feeling.

Still, Jeff tried to put aside his emotions and get to work. But he made sure Rebecca was kept busy. Too busy to be available for any flirting with Bill.

EVERYTHING WAS GOING SMOOTHLY. Rebecca was working diligently at the sudden increase of duties she'd received since Jeff returned to work.

He'd offered to take them to the zoo on Saturday. Again Rebecca had tried to convince her son that her presence wasn't necessary, but Joey had disagreed with her and so had Jeff.

Rebecca worried that she wasn't fighting hard enough. She knew she wanted to be with Jeff, but she had to realize he was engaged to Chelsea. Her son had a role in Jeff's life, but Rebecca didn't, and she tried to remind herself of that fact at every turn.

Then Thursday afternoon came and all hell broke loose....

"Rebecca, you have a call...and the woman sounds upset," Harriet warned as she held out the phone for Rebecca.

"Hello?"

"Hi, it's Betty. Peter was playing ball with Joey and—and it was an accident, but the ball hit him in the mouth. Oh, Rebecca, it knocked his tooth out! We didn't know what to do. I wrapped the tooth in a cold wet cloth, but who do we take him to?"

"I don't know, but I'll be right there," she promised, and hung up the phone. "Sorry, Harriet, but Joey's been hurt. I have to leave."

"Jeff will drive you."

"No, that's not necessary," she protested, grabbing her purse and hurrying to the door.

Jeff came out of his office. "Did you call me, Harriet? Where's Rebecca going?"

"Joey's been hurt. She's going home."

"Does she have her car here?"

"No, she walked, as usual. I said you would drive her but she said it wasn't necessary."

"Take care of things," Jeff ordered over his shoulder as he hurried after Rebecca.

AN HOUR LATER, CHELSEA arrived at the office. Jeff had said he would take her to the French restaurant they'd skipped Monday evening.

She was not happy to discover that her fiancé had left with Rebecca because Joey had gotten hurt. When she expressed her displeasure, Harriet asked, "Shall I call Rebecca's house and see if they can tell me when Jeff will return?"

"Of course I want you to do that!" Chelsea snapped. She paced the office as Harriet made the call.

"I see," Harriet said into the phone. "Will you have him call the office as soon as you hear from him? Yes, thank you."

Chelsea stared at her. "Well?"

"He and Rebecca took Joey to Jeff's dentist, but

they have to wait until he's dealt with his other patients. They're not sure when he'll be back.''

"And I'm supposed to hang around waiting for him?"

Bill stepped out of his office. "What's wrong?"

Harriet explained the problem while Chelsea frowned at him.

"That's too bad. How about I take you to the coffee shop until Jeff can get back? Give your cell phone number to Harriet and she'll call as soon as she gets some news. Isn't that right, Harriet?"

"Yes, of course," Harriet agreed readily.

"Good. Come along, Chelsea, my girl. We could both use a cup of coffee today."

And with that, Chelsea found herself swept out the door, much to Harriet's relief.

JEFF AND REBECCA SAT with Joey between them. He leaned against his mother most of the time, but Jeff kept a hand on his shoulder. "Are you hanging in there, Joey?" he asked.

As Betty had said, Joey's tooth was wrapped in ice, and Joey held a bag of ice on his mouth, too. He lowered the ice. "Sure. It doesn't hurt much."

"Keep the ice on your mouth, sweetie," Rebecca said, squeezing Joey's hand. "It shouldn't be much longer."

"No, it shouldn't since Dr. John's last patient went in half an hour ago. Then we'll find out what can be done for your tooth, Joey."

"I'm sure it was a baby tooth," Rebecca said

again, as she had several times earlier. "His adult teeth won't come in for a couple of years."

"We'll wait and let Dr. John decide that." Jeff stretched out his legs, trying to ease the tension he felt. He'd found it more difficult to withstand Joey's pain than anything he'd ever suffered himself, including a broken bone when he was playing football in high school.

The nurse returned to the waiting room to call Joey in. Both Rebecca and Jeff got up and accompanied him to the door.

"Hello, Jeff," the man in a white coat said in greeting. "Why don't you introduce us?"

"Sure. This is my son, Joey, and his mother, Rebecca Barlow."

"Hello. I'm Dr. John Ballard. Now, let's see what happened, Joey. Can you smile for me?"

Joey took down the ice pack and bravely tried to smile.

The dentist patted Joey's back. "Good try. Now I'm going to lift your lip, okay?"

Joey nodded.

The doctor looked at Joey's gums. Then he asked if the tooth had been saved.

Rebecca handed him the tooth wrapped in a clean cloth and buried in a bag of ice.

Dr. Ballard set the bag of ice down on a nearby table, withdrew the cloth and unwrapped the tooth. "This is a baby tooth. There doesn't appear to be any damage to his gums or any future teeth. His replacement tooth might not come as soon as we'd like, but it will come in."

"Is there anything we should do?" Rebecca asked anxiously.

"You might give him some children's Tylenol to ease the pain, and use ice until the swelling of his lips goes down. If he continues to have pain, call me."

"Thank you for seeing us today," Rebecca said with a genuine smile.

"Yeah, John, we appreciate it," Jeff added.

"You might want to get his teeth cleaned in six months or so. Give my nurse a call."

After they left the dentist's office, Rebecca said, "I like him. I may start going to see him, too."

"He's married." Jeff was trying to eliminate the dentist from any potential flirting with Rebecca, just as he had Bill.

Rebecca gasped. "Should that make a difference?"

"I just wanted you to know," he said, shrugging his shoulders, hoping she wouldn't guess his reasoning.

"All right."

They got into Jeff's car and rode silently back to Vivian's home. Jeff got out of the car with them and came in. As soon as everyone knew they were back, they crowded around Joey as if he were returning from war.

Betty offered Joey a bowl of ice cream. Peter offered to do anything Joey wanted. Vivian was sure he needed to go to bed at once. Will promised to teach him how to avoid such pain in the future, and Vanessa was giving him kisses.

"I feel totally useless," Jeff muttered.

"You weren't useless at the doctor's office," Rebecca told him. "That's the first time I've had someone to rely on when we had an emergency. I appreciate it."

"Have you had a lot of emergencies?"

"Once, when he was eighteen months, he swallowed a penny. Another night, he ran a very high fever, and I had to take him to the emergency room because I was afraid he had some horrible disease. The waiting is painful when you're the only adult, and you're not sure if you're doing the right thing."

"I'm sorry I wasn't there with you."

"Well, we both know that's my fault." She moved away to stop the conversation. "I think Joey needs to go to bed, and I'll bring him up a tray of food. Maybe a grilled cheese sandwich and some tomato soup, Betty, if that's possible?"

"'Course it is. I'll have it ready in fifteen minutes."

"Thank you so much. Tell everyone good-night, sweetie."

"But, Mommy, I think I should get to watch television," Joey informed her.

Rebecca didn't get angry. She just smiled and said, "And I think you should do as I said. Up the stairs and into your jammies."

He gave in easily, which showed her how tired he really was. Trauma always wears out a person.

"May I help you put on your pajamas and get ready for bed?" Jeff asked.

"Hey, yeah, 'cause we're both boys," Joey agreed, intrigued with that idea. "Mommy, can he help me?"

"Of course. That would be nice. I'll go find your pajamas while you wash your face and hands."

The three of them left the family and climbed the stairs. "I can see why Joey might be spoiled a little. They're very loving," Jeff said.

"I don't think you can have too much loving. When we lived in Arkansas, there was only me and Joey, and Mrs. Button, who baby-sat him. We've really enjoyed having family here."

"I know what you mean. I haven't had any family since my uncle died. At least none that I knew of."

Rebecca refused to say anything else about their situation. Joey and his dad took a long time in the bathroom. Rebecca handed in the clean pajamas. Then she told them she was going down to get Joey's dinner.

When she came back up with the tray, Joey was in bed and Jeff was reading him one of his favorite books. She waited until Jeff finished the book. Then she asked him to pile up the pillows so Joey could eat. They both teased him into eating most of his dinner.

Rebecca gave him two children's Tylenol tablets and watched his eyelids grow heavy. She kissed him good-night and encouraged him to hug his daddy's neck. Then she told him she would leave the light on in the bathroom and he should call her if he needed her.

"Maybe I should stay. I could sleep in the other bed in his room so he won't bother you."

"He won't bother me. I said that so he'd know he wasn't alone, but he's going to sleep well tonight."

"I feel like I'm not being very helpful."

"I told you I appreciated your going with us to the dentist. That helped a lot."

As they came down the stairs, Betty came running down the hall. "Mr. Jacobs! I forgot to tell you to call your office when you got back. Your fiancée was there waiting for you."

"Oh, I'm sorry, Jeff. You shouldn't have gone with us. I didn't know you had a date with Chelsea." Rebecca felt terribly guilty.

"Damn! May I use your phone?" he asked Betty.

"Of course you can. And Miz Vivian said to ask you to stay for dinner. It will be ready in five minutes."

"Let me see how things stand with Chelsea. Then I'll let you know."

Rebecca was going to excuse herself, but Jeff caught her hand and stopped her from leaving the library. "Chelsea? I hope Harriet told you about the emergency." He stood listening for several minutes. Rebecca looked away. "I see. Well, then, I'll see you Saturday morning. I'll pick you up at nine, okay?"

After a brief moment, he hung up the phone. "That's interesting," he said.

That remark got her attention. ''What was interesting?''

''It appears Bill took Chelsea out to dinner and then took her home. Her only complaint is that he refused to kiss her good-night.''

Chapter Four

"Doesn't that upset you?" Rebecca asked with concern.

"No." He grinned. "That's Chelsea trying to pay me back for not keeping our date."

"Oh."

"Am I still invited to dinner?" he asked when she said nothing else.

"Oh! Yes, of course. Let's go find the others."

Rebecca thought it would be best for her to see Jeff only in the company of others. She was too drawn to him, remembering the past, wanting a future that could never be.

Will stood up as they came into the library, and shook Jeff's hand. Vivian made him feel welcome.

"How are things going between you and Joey? He's such a sweet boy!"

"Fine, Vivian. It will just take a little time to make up for four years." He looked at Rebecca and held up a hand in apology, like tennis players do when the ball hits the net and goes over to the other player's side, giving his opponent a point.

"Rebecca has done a good job of raising him," Jeff added.

"Yes, she has. And he's so smart. Smart children are more difficult to raise. Vanessa could always think of a good excuse to do what she wanted," Vivian said with a laugh.

"I can imagine," Jeff agreed as Vanessa protested.

"Dinner's ready," Betty announced as she entered the room.

They all went in to dinner. Jeff took the seat beside Rebecca.

She was a nervous wreck, finding it difficult to eat with Jeff sitting beside her, making conversation with Will. It seemed Jeff had a client who could use Will's services.

When dinner was over, Jeff asked Rebecca if they could check on Joey one more time, to be sure he'd gotten to sleep.

They went up the stairs and opened Joey's door quietly. The little boy was curled up under the covers, clutching his favorite teddy bear, sound asleep.

"Does he always sleep with his teddy bear?" Jeff asked after they'd closed the door.

"Yes. He sometimes gets scared in the dark. The teddy bear makes him feel better." She thought maybe he was disappointed that his son wasn't brave. "When he gets older, he won't need the teddy bear, I'm sure."

"It doesn't matter. I just wish I'd been there those times he got scared."

She turned her back to him. "It always comes down to my mistake, doesn't it?"

"I'm sorry. But it hurts that you didn't think I'd care."

"Jeff—I was in shock when I first found out. My parents' reaction made it worse. It seemed like no one cared and it was just me and the baby, on our own. Afterward, after Joey was born, I was afraid to let go, to bring someone else in to our close-knit world. It was wrong, I know, but I told you as soon as I found you."

"You didn't exactly look for me."

"I know. What do you want me to do to make up for my negligence?"

Suddenly, he pulled her into his arms and kissed her. The kiss went on and on. She knew it was wrong, but she couldn't pull away. She'd been longing for him to touch her for five years.

When he finally released her, she stared at him in shock.

"I shouldn't have done that. I'm sorry." He backed away from her, his hands in the air in surrender. "You're just so damned tempting!"

"So this is my fault, too?"

He gave her a rueful grin. "No, honey, it's my fault because I have no resistance. I never did have when it came to you. That's why we have a son upstairs." He took another step back. "I'm going now. I'll see you tomorrow at work."

He left at once, as if he was afraid someone would chase him away. Rebecca leaned against the closed door, savoring the kiss she'd dreamed of so many times. She smiled—reality was even better.

IT WAS IRONIC, JEFF THOUGHT. Chelsea tried to threaten him with a kiss, and he'd taken that thought and made his own mistake. And it had been a mistake. Now, every time he saw Rebecca, he would remember that kiss and yearn for more.

He finally had to face the fact that his feelings for Chelsea were nothing compared to what he had felt for Rebecca years ago and still felt for her now.

But he had committed himself to Chelsea.

If he were a drinking man, tonight would be the perfect time to drink himself senseless. Unfortunately, he wasn't. He would have to deal with the situation in another way.

And the first thing he had to do was call Chelsea and apologize.

REBECCA TRIED TO TELL Jeff she and Joey would meet them at the zoo Saturday morning. Jeff wouldn't agree to that. "No, we'll pick you up at nine o'clock. Well, actually about ten after. I'm picking Chelsea up at nine."

"All right. Did she forgive you for last night?"

"Yes, sort of. And I thanked Bill for entertaining her."

"Did I hear my name mentioned?" Bill Wallace asked as he came to the door of his office.

"I was just telling Rebecca that I thanked you for taking Chelsea to dinner last night."

"But I told you you didn't have to thank me. Chelsea was a lot of fun."

"And you like French food?" Jeff asked.

"Oh, we didn't go to that restaurant. I took her to a good steak place."

"Chelsea refuses to eat at a steak house," Jeff said, frowning.

"Well, I really didn't give her a choice. I had no intention of eating strange food while some snooty maître d' stared down his nose at me. It would give me heartburn."

"I'm glad you enjoyed your meal," Jeff said, still frowning.

Rebecca turned back to her work. She didn't want to know if Chelsea threw a temper tantrum.

Jeff stood there, his hands on his hips.

"She didn't complain?" he asked Bill.

"Sure she did. But I teased her out of her bad mood."

"I guess I never tried that." Jeff shrugged his shoulders.

"No, because it's easier to give in. You've got to think about how things will be after you marry Chelsea, Jeff. Are you sure you're doing the right thing?"

Jeff ran his fingers through his dark hair. "Bill, I can't discuss my marriage with you."

"Okay. Well, you don't owe me thanks for last night. I enjoyed myself."

JEFF PICKED CHELSEA UP at nine o'clock, as promised. Or, at least, he arrived at that time. She wasn't quite ready, and he was invited in to have a cup of coffee with Chelsea's father.

"You know, Jeff, I'm so glad to have Chelsea's future settled. She's not one of these career types. She's like her mother. She'll run your life for you, which will do wonders for your career."

Jeff suppressed the urge to tell Mr. Wexham that he didn't want Chelsea running his life. Just then, Chelsea bounced into the room, a huge smile on her face. "Sorry I'm late, Jeff."

She looked about sixteen, dressed in overall shorts and a T-shirt. In fact, Jeff had never seen her look so casual. Or so happy.

Once they were in the car, he observed, "I should take you to the zoo once a month if it makes you this happy."

"Silly, it's not the zoo. We, Mom and I, went shopping for my wedding gown yesterday and I fell in love with one. Mom said I could have it. Dad almost swallowed his teeth, but it's worth every penny. After all, it's a Vera Wang."

"Um, is the groom allowed to ask how much it cost?"

"Probably not, but I don't mind telling. We got a bargain. It was just under twenty!"

"Twenty dollars?"

Chelsea stared at him. "You're joking, right?"

"The only other thing that fits is thousand and that would mean—you spent twenty thousand on the wedding dress!"

"Well, it is the most important part of the wedding.

The wedding cake is second, of course, and we put our order in as soon as we got engaged.''

''Six months ago?''

''Oh, yes. There's only one decorator who makes the best cakes. Mine will have blossoms that spill down the five layers. It'll be the most beautiful thing, almost too pretty to eat.''

''And it's going to cost, what, a couple of hundred?''

''No. The main cake itself is seventy-five hundred, but we'll need additional cakes to serve all our guests, so it'll be about ten thousand.''

''And I don't suppose you considered cutting the guest list?''

''Actually, I did. The caterers were outrageous!''

''I thought we were serving cake?''

''Well, of course, but you have to have real food, too. Nowadays, you have stations. A roast beef station, a shrimp station, a roast-of-lamb station. Some weddings divide their stations by carrying different ethnic foods. Greek, Mexican, French, American, but I don't think that's as elegant. And of course, at each station, you have a mix of vegetables and finger foods.''

Jeff wasn't quite grasping what Chelsea was saying. He was too preoccupied with arriving at Rebecca's home. ''We're here. Do you want to come in or wait in the car?'' Jeff was glad to change the subject. The thought of the cost and planning of the wedding was making him sick.

"Oh, I'll come in. I had no idea they lived so well."

"This is Vivian Greenfield's house, Chelsea, not Rebecca's."

"I should've known."

Jeff raised his eyebrows. He didn't hold out much hope for the day ahead of him. When he rang the doorbell, Betty answered, but Joey was right behind her.

"Hi! We're ready. We're going to see lions, Betty!"

"I know, Joey. You've been growling at me all morning. Come on in, Mr. Jacobs, you and your friend."

"Betty, this is my fiancée, Chelsea Wexham."

In response, Betty smiled and offered a hand in welcome. Chelsea stared first at Jeff and then at Betty's hand, as if she didn't know what to do about it. Finally, at the very last minute, she barely shook Betty's hand.

"Have you had breakfast, 'cause I can fix something real quick. It's best to start out with a full stomach," Betty offered as she led them to the library.

"We've eaten, Betty, thank you. How about you, Joey? Have you eaten?" Jeff smiled at the little boy who was dancing around in excitement.

"I ate twice. First, when Betty fixed my breakfast. Then I helped Mommy eat her breakfast."

"That was mighty good of you. Did Mommy say thank you?"

"Yes. But she said I mustn't eat too much or they might want to eat me up!"

"Who might want to?"

"The lions and tigers, a'course!"

"Good thing Mommy warned you," Jeff said, grinning at the nonsense.

Chelsea, however, wasn't charmed. "Don't be ridiculous. They don't feed children to the lions and tigers!" she snapped.

Before Jeff could think of a subtle reprimand, his son spoke.

"I know, Chelsea. Mommy was making a joke because I'm excited to go to the zoo."

Having life explained to her by an almost four-year-old left Chelsea with nothing to say.

Jeff winked at Joey. "Is your mom ready to go?"

"She's on her way down," Betty said, having gone upstairs to let Rebecca know they were there. Rebecca came down wearing jeans and a sweater, much as she'd been dressed Monday night.

She greeted Jeff and Chelsea, adding a compliment about Chelsea's overalls.

"Thank you. Someone told me that I was too pretentious, so I thought I'd give overalls a try." Her expression was triumphant, but Jeff knew he hadn't made that remark, so who was she planning to show?

"And they have big pockets for peanuts to feed the elephants!" Joey added knowledgeably. "On TV I saw an elephant who could get the peanuts out of your pocket with his long nose without you doing anything!"

"That's called his trunk, Joey, not his nose," Rebecca corrected.

"But it's just like a nose," Jeff said, "and I'd like to see the elephant do that to Chelsea. Wouldn't you, Chelsea?"

"Absolutely not! You're both being silly. Let's go." She turned around and marched back down the hall to the front door.

Jeff looked at Rebecca, wondering if she understood his fiancée any better than he did. But she shrugged her shoulders and caught Joey's hand in hers. "We're ready."

In the car, Chelsea chattered nonstop about the plans for their wedding. Joey almost fell asleep in the back seat, since he had no interest in the conversation. Chelsea, however, thought of a role for him.

"Jeff, Joey can be the ring-bearer. I didn't have any cousins or friends with children young enough to be cute. But Joey would be perfect. He'll look darling in a tux."

"Just when is the wedding?" Rebecca asked.

"In June, of course. It's the perfect month for a wedding."

"But how long have you been engaged?"

"We got engaged last March," Chelsea said. "And I thought about getting married last June, but I didn't want my wedding to be all harum-scarum. It takes time to have a perfect wedding. And three months just wasn't enough time to plan my dream wedding. I was telling Jeff earlier, the cake had to be ordered months in advance, and I just found my dress yesterday. It's a Vera Wang. But it will have to be made to my measurements, of course.''

''It's not ready-made? I mean, you can't buy it and take it home with you?''

''A Vera Wang? Well, I suppose she does some pret-a-porter, but I want one made strictly for me.''

''I see.''

''Look—there's a giant giraffe!'' Joey screamed.

''He's a statue, sweetie,'' Rebecca told her little boy.

''Yeah, Joey, he guards the entrance so we can find it easily,'' Jeff told him. ''If you get lost, just look around and go to the giant giraffe.''

''Oh,'' Joey said in a long, drawn-out breath.

Chelsea, too, seemed impressed with the giraffe. Suddenly she was sitting up straighter in her seat, craning her neck to see it.

''Haven't you seen the giraffe before, Chelsea?'' Jeff asked out of curiosity.

''Yes, of course, but it's been a long time.'' She continued to stare, but she tried to look nonchalant. Jeff parked the car, and they all got out to walk to the entrance.

After Jeff bought the tickets, they moved inside the walls of the zoo, where the giant giraffe stood.

''Why, I believe that's Bill over there!'' Chelsea exclaimed.

Startled, Jeff looked up in time to see his partner walking toward them.

''Bill? What are you doing here?'' he asked in surprise.

"Didn't Chelsea tell you? She invited me."

Jeff and Rebecca turned to stare at Chelsea.

"Well, Jeff spends all his time with his kid, and Rebecca doesn't mind, but I don't like to be ignored. I thought Bill could keep me company."

Jeff let out a deep breath. "I think it would've been polite to at least tell me Bill was going to be joining us, Chelsea."

"I thought you'd say no."

Jeff knew that this wasn't the time or the place to address this. Besides, he didn't want to make a scene in front of Rebecca, Joey or Bill. Instead he just shook his head. "Of course you're welcome to join us, Bill. Joey and I plan to find the elephant that can get peanuts out of Chelsea's pockets." He grabbed Joey's hand and headed in the direction of the elephant house, warning Joey to keep his eyes peeled for a place they could buy peanuts.

REBECCA THOUGHT THE DAY at the zoo was turning out to be a lot of fun after the bizarre start. And Chelsea was right. Bill fit right in and entertained Chelsea when the other two adults were involved with Joey.

Joey was having the time of his life. His father was spoiling him rotten. He'd had peanuts, cotton candy, chocolate candy and several colas. Now Jeff was announcing they needed to stop for lunch.

To no one's surprise, Joey said he wasn't hungry.

"That's because your father has been feeding you junk food all morning," Rebecca said.

Joey, sitting beside his mother, tugged on her

shoulder and whispered, "I don't think they know, Mommy."

"Know what?" Rebecca whispered in return.

"About him being my daddy. He may want to keep it secret."

"Is that why you never call him Daddy?"

Joey nodded his head.

Rebecca had noticed the way her son avoided calling Jeff Daddy or even by his first name. She had started to say something several times, but she hadn't wanted to embarrass Jeff or Joey. Instead, she bent over to kiss her son to show him she understood and cared.

"What is it?" Jeff asked, his face showing obvious concern.

"Joey was warning me not to call you his father in front of the others in case you were trying to keep it a secret."

"Mommy!" Joey protested.

"Joey, they already know I'm your daddy," Jeff said hurriedly.

"I think that may be why he's never called you Daddy, either," Rebecca added, staring at her son with tears in her eyes.

"Is that true, Joey?" Jeff asked.

"I didn't know if you'd like it," Joey said, staring down at his athletic shoes, too embarrassed to look up at Jeff.

"We should've talked about this before now. It's my fault. I didn't want to rush you about calling me

Daddy. I'd love for you to call me Daddy, but if you don't want to, you can call me Jeff.''

This time Joey looked up at Jeff. "Are you sure?"

"I'm very sure."

"Then I'd like to call you Daddy."

Jeff picked him up and hugged him tight against him. "Boy, that sure sounds wonderful coming from you."

"What a touching moment," Chelsea said with a lot of sarcasm.

Bill stood, took Chelsea's arm and practically dragged her away from the table.

Jeff paid them no attention. "I'm glad we've got that settled, Joey. I was afraid you didn't like me."

"Aw, Daddy, I always like people who buy me peanuts, popcorn, candy and colas."

It took Jeff a moment to realize his almost-four-year-old was teasing him. When he finally figured it out, he grabbed Joey and began tickling him. Joey was shrieking with great joy.

Just as Rebecca was calling the two males in her life to order, Bill and Chelsea came back to the table. Much to everyone's surprise, Chelsea apologized to Jeff if she'd seemed insensitive a few minutes ago.

Jeff stared at her blankly, not really sure if she was being sincere or if Bill was forcing her to apologize.

"Well, it makes you sound so old," Chelsea said, trying to explain her behavior.

"So I guess you don't want Joey to call you Mommy?" Jeff asked with a grin.

It was hard to determine which one looked more horrified, Joey or Chelsea.

"Daddy was just teasing, Joey," Rebecca said quietly.

Her words reassured Chelsea, also.

"He can call me Chelsea."

"And if you keep on wearing those overalls," Bill pointed out, "in a few years they'll think he's your date instead of your stepson!"

Chelsea burst into tears and ran away from the table. Both men looked helplessly at Rebecca. She got up from the table and followed Chelsea over to a tree under which she was standing.

"Chelsea, what's wrong?"

Chelsea hurriedly rubbed away her tears. "Nothing I care to discuss with you."

"Bill was just pointing out how young and cute you look in the overalls. I'm sure he didn't mean any harm," Rebecca offered, despite Chelsea's rude comment.

"Are you sure? I—I bought these overalls because Bill said I didn't know how to dress for fun. And then I thought he was making fun of me."

"That would upset me, too," Rebecca assured her with a smile. "But I'm sure that's not what he was doing." She looked over at the others. "Let's go back to the table. They can't go get our food until we're there to stay with Joey."

"But how will I explain my tears?"

"Oh, Chelsea, never explain. We don't want them to think they can figure us out."

A look of realization shone in Chelsea's eyes. "Yes, of course. What a good idea."

They walked back to the table. When both men questioned her, she smiled and said, "I had a headache."

Both men looked dumbfounded.

"I think you'd better get in line for our hamburgers. There's a big crowd coming," Rebecca pointed out with a smile.

The men hurried away, fear of standing in a long line making them rush to the hamburger stand.

"Well, that went well," Rebecca said with a grin at Chelsea.

"Thank you, Rebecca," Chelsea said slowly, as if the words were hard for her to say. "My mother would've insisted on a detailed explanation that would've embarrassed me."

"Good heavens, with that to look forward to, you must hide all your emotions."

"Mostly," Chelsea admitted with a shrug. "Mother doesn't like tears."

"I think they're therapeutic, sometimes."

"I like that idea. You have a great way of explaining things. I'll have to remember to say that to my mother."

Rebecca grinned. "Just don't attach my name to it."

Chelsea giggled. "You're a lot of fun...for a mother."

Chapter Five

"So, Chelsea, you're going to be a stepmother. Are you all right with that?" Rebecca asked. She knew she shouldn't be prying into Jeff's business, but as Joey's mother, she felt she had a right to know. Chelsea mostly seemed to ignore Joey, and that worried Rebecca.

Chelsea shrugged her shoulders. "I don't suppose I'll be around your little boy that much. I mean, Jeff will most likely spend time alone with him doing boy things."

Rebecca hesitated, but she couldn't leave things as they were, especially if Chelsea was going to be a part of her son's future. "Do you not like little boys?"

Chelsea looked shocked. "I don't dislike them. I've just never been around them. I don't know what to do with them."

"Well, I could teach you about little boys and what they like to do, so when you become Joey's stepmother, it won't frighten you."

"I didn't say it frightened me," Chelsea said, her eyes round and accusing.

"I'm sorry. I just thought— Hmm. I just know from my own experience, when I don't know about something, it tends to frighten me. I wasn't trying to make a judgment about your character or mothering skills," Rebecca said gently.

"Oh." Chelsea relaxed and seemed a little less defensive. "I guess it does rather scare me a little. I don't know what small boys like."

"I like hamburgers," Joey said helpfully, watching Chelsea. Then he looked up and saw his father and Bill. "Here they are, Mommy. Hurray! They got french fries, too!"

"Now you know what little boys like," Rebecca said with a laugh. "But that doesn't mean he shouldn't eat vegetables as well."

Chelsea grinned. "I'll remember."

The two men reached the table with two trays loaded with food. In the flurry of distributing everyone's meals, Jeff stole a look at Rebecca. "Everything okay?"

"Yes, everything's fine." And it was. Rebecca had discovered that Chelsea wasn't as pretentious and cold as she'd thought. She just hadn't had any experience with children, and she was frightened by the unknown. Maybe Rebecca could help Chelsea get to know Joey, so that when Joey spent time with Chelsea and Jeff, it wouldn't torture Rebecca with fears of neglect or mistreatment.

When they all finally left the zoo, Rebecca felt it

had been a day well spent. But she was exhausted, as was Joey. He'd fallen asleep on Jeff's shoulder as he carried him to the car.

Bill interrupted Jeff's attempt to get everyone in his car. "Jeff, why don't you let me take Chelsea home so you can get Joey to bed as soon as possible? The little guy is obviously really tired from his full day of excitement."

"Chelsea, do you mind? Joey needs to get to his bed for a little sleep before dinner," Jeff said, concentrating on his son.

"That will be fine," Chelsea agreed calmly.

Rebecca watched Chelsea, amazed that it didn't bother her that she was being passed off to Bill because of Joey. Rebecca wanted to tell Jeff that wasn't smart, but before she could decide what to do, she found herself in the front seat next to Jeff, with Joey asleep on the back seat, belted in.

As they drove, Rebecca finally said, "Jeff, I don't think it's a good idea to shuffle Chelsea off to Bill. She may blame Joey for separating the two of you."

Jeff turned to stare at her until traffic demanded he pay attention to his driving. "Chelsea understands that I need this time to bond and form a relationship with Joey. Otherwise she would've thrown a fit. Overall, I think things went well today."

"Yes, they did. I didn't expect to like Chelsea, but I do. I see why you like Chelsea and chose her for your wife-to-be. I'm going to teach her about little boys, so Joey won't frighten her."

"You could teach me, too."

Rebecca looked at him, sure he was teasing her. When he appeared to be serious, she said, "You don't need any teaching. You seem to know what to do instinctively. Joey has taken a real liking to you, and you didn't seem to be struggling with what to do next with him."

"He's a smart little boy. Happy, too. You've done a good job, Becca. You could've taught him to hate me, since I wasn't around, but you didn't do that. I really appreciate that."

"Why would I do that? It would only hurt Joey." To say nothing of herself. She didn't want Joey to hate Jeff. She couldn't hate him, either.

Jeff parked his car in front of Vivian's house. "I'll carry Joey up to his room."

Rebecca followed him into the house, waving to Betty as she admitted them. Upstairs, Rebecca turned back the bedcovers and helped Jeff put Joey in bed. The little boy never opened his eyes.

"He had a wonderful time today, Jeff. Thank you," she whispered.

"It was my pleasure," he assured her as they left Joey's room. "And you? Did you have a good time as well?"

She could only answer honestly. "I did. Bill and Chelsea are both nice people. I enjoyed getting to know them better very much."

"I had a nice time, too."

By that time, they'd reached the bottom of the stairs. Vivian appeared and asked Jeff to stay for dinner.

"I don't want to put you to any trouble, Vivian," Jeff said.

"Don't be silly. Betty always makes too much food, anyway. Besides, we're celebrating tonight."

"Oh? What are we celebrating?" Rebecca asked in surprise.

Vivian's cheeks flushed. "I can't tell you yet. We're waiting for Vanessa to come home. She's been at the library all day working on a paper."

"Well, with that kind of enticement, how can I do anything but accept your invitation to dinner, Vivian? If you're sure I won't be intruding?"

"Oh, no. You will need to know, anyway, Jeff. It's just so exciting!" Vivian gushed, her cheeks again red. Then she swayed slightly.

Rebecca reached out and took her arms. "Are you all right, Vivian?"

"I just felt a little dizzy for a moment. I'm fine."

"Let's go sit down, Vivian. Where's Will?" Jeff put an arm around Vivian's shoulders and led her toward the library.

Rebecca slipped away to the kitchen to check with Betty about Jeff staying for dinner. "Um, Betty, do you know what we're celebrating tonight?"

"No. Miz Vivian said it was a secret, but she sure seemed excited."

"Yes, she is. I think I'll try to call Vanessa on her cell phone."

Rebecca picked up the phone and dialed Vanessa's cell phone number by memory. When her sister answered, Rebecca asked, "When are you coming home, Vanessa?"

"Oh, Rebecca, I was thinking about going to get some dinner with—with Jeremy. Would you tell Mom?"

"No, Vanessa, I think you should come home. Your mom is real excited and says we're celebrating tonight."

"What are we celebrating?"

"I don't know. She wouldn't tell me. She wanted to wait for you to come home before she makes her big announcement. She'd be awfully disappointed if you didn't come home tonight for dinner."

"Okay. I can go out with Jeremy another time. I'll be home in fifteen minutes."

"Good. I'll tell Betty." After she hung up the phone, she let Betty know that Vanessa would be home in a few minutes. Then she went to the library, where Jeff had taken Vivian.

"I just talked to Vanessa. She said she'd be home in fifteen minutes," Rebecca announced as she sat down.

"Oh, good. I'm so excited, I can't wait!" Vivian exclaimed. Will got up from behind his desk and sat down on the sofa next to his wife.

"I think you'd better calm down or I'll have to send you upstairs to bed."

His threat didn't seem to upset Vivian. She snuggled up next to him, still beaming with happiness.

"I'll be good," Vivian promised.

Betty came in with a tray of hors d'oeuvres.

"Thought you might be hungry. These will keep you from starving."

After Betty had left the room, Jeff looked at Will. "How do the ladies of the house stay so slender?"

Will shrugged his shoulders. "I don't know. I'm trying to be careful myself, but Betty just keeps bringing delicious food, just in case we're starving."

After a few more minutes of chitchat, they all heard Vanessa's voice in the hallway. Vivian leaped to her feet, but Will kept her from running to her daughter. "In here, Vanessa," he called.

Jeff stood as Vanessa came into the room, and so did Rebecca.

"Hi, everyone. Did I hold up dinner?" Vanessa asked as she entered the room.

"No," Will assured her. "But your mom was getting a little impatient."

"I'm sorry, Mom. I could've—"

"Will's just teasing me, darling. But we do have exciting news. I wanted to wait until you were here to tell everyone." Vivian's cheeks were bright red.

"Well, I'm here now. What's the big news?"

"Vanessa, you know I love you more than anything even though I didn't actually give birth to you?"

"Of course I do, Mom."

"And I told you God gave you to me because I couldn't have my own baby?"

Vanessa nodded, frowning now.

"Well, we were wrong. I can have my own baby."

Vanessa stared at her mother, waiting for more explanation.

Rebecca, however, had figured out what Vivian meant. "No! Really?" She jumped up and hugged Vivian. "I'm so happy for the two of you. Are you feeling all right?"

"Why would you ask—Mom? You're pregnant? We're going to have a baby? I can't believe it. Are you sure?"

Vivian nodded, beaming at her daughter.

"You've seen a doctor? He says everything is okay?" Jeff asked.

"Yes. I'm only forty-three, Jeff. Other women have had a baby at my age. Usually not their first one, I'll admit, but so far everything's fine, and the doctors are going to watch my pregnancy very closely." Vivian shared a look with Will. "We're so excited."

"It's hard to believe that I'm going to be changing diapers at this stage of my life," Will said with a big grin.

"You'll be a great father, Will," Vanessa told her stepfather. "Do you know if it is a boy or a girl? Are you going to find out?"

"It's too early to tell. Your mom and I don't care which one it is, honey. If it's half as good as you, we'll be satisfied," Will assured her.

Vanessa hugged Will's neck and then her mother's. "I'm so excited that we're going to have a baby. After all these years of hoping, it's finally come true. I've already got Rebecca, and hopefully more siblings as soon as we find them. Now I can have another sister or brother.''

Betty entered the room. "Dinner is ready."

"Betty, I can tell you our news now," Vivian said, watching her housekeeper closely. "We're going to have a baby."

Betty's look swung first from Vanessa to Rebecca. "Who is?"

"I am," Vivian said, beaming at Betty.

Betty practically went into hysterics, screaming and hugging Vivian. She immediately summoned Peter from the kitchen so that he, too, could share in their happiness. It was several minutes before dinner was served.

Joey didn't awaken until almost eight o'clock. Betty fed him leftovers in the kitchen. The rest of the family sat in the library and talked about the new baby soon to join their family.

"Have you thought of names yet?" Jeff asked.

"We'll probably wait until we know the sex of the baby. That way we'll only have to make one list of names," Will told him.

"Good thinking. I believe choosing a name is one of the hardest parts about having a baby."

Vivian's face filled with concern. "You didn't get the chance to name Joey, did you?"

"No, but I couldn't have chosen a better name. You see, Rebecca named him after me and my dad."

"She did?" Vivian asked, sending a loving smile toward Rebecca.

"My dad's name was Joseph, and my middle name

is Lee. Joey is named Joseph Lee. The only thing we have to change is the last name.''

Rebecca appeared startled by his remark.

''What are you planning?'' Will asked.

''I want his last name to be Jacobs. After all, we share responsibility for him now. But Rebecca and I will have to discuss it later.''

It was as if the two men were having a private conversation. Vivian looked at Rebecca and shrugged.

''I'll see if Joey's finished eating. Then we can tell him your good news, Vivian,'' Rebecca said, slipping into the kitchen.

A couple of minutes later, she brought Joey into the room. ''Joey, Grandpa Will and Grandma Vivian have some exciting news for you.''

''They do? Are we going to get a pet elephant?'' the little boy asked, looking around excitedly.

Vanessa stared at her nephew. ''Why would you ask that, Joey?''

''Well, we saw the elephants today, and I think I'd like to have a pet elephant.''

''They're not allowed in our neighborhood,'' Will said solemnly.

''Oh. Then what is the good news?''

Vivian leaned forward. ''Grandpa and I are going to have a baby, Joey. In a few months, you'll have a new baby to play with.''

Joey frowned. ''Are they fun to play with?''

Will burst out laughing.

Jeff swung his child up into his arms. ''I guess we'll find out together, son. But you should congratulate your grandparents on their good news about the baby.''

"Okay. Congratulations, Grandpa Will and Grandma Vivian.''

"Thank you, Joey,'' Will said for both of them. Vivian smiled at Joey. "I think the baby will be fun for you, Joey, and your daddy, because you won't be expected to change diapers,'' she said.

"Eeew,'' Joey returned, making a terrible face.

"That's not polite, Joey,'' Rebecca said softly.

"But, Mommy, dirty diapers aren't polite, either.''

"He has a point,'' Will agreed. "I think we need to talk about having someone to play ball with. In two or three years, Joey, our baby will be able to play ball with you.''

"That'll be neat,'' Joey agreed, "but how long do I have to wait?''

"Maybe when you're seven,'' Vivian said. "Our baby will be three and that's old enough to play ball.''

Joey's enthusiasm diminished somewhat. "When I'm seven? That's really old. And that's a long time to wait. Waiting is hard. I don't think I can wait that long.

Rebecca laughed with everyone else, but she told her son it was his bedtime. After he'd told everyone good-night, she took his hand and led him upstairs. Jeff followed.

"Can I help tuck Joey into bed again tonight?'' he asked Rebecca.

"I suppose, if you want.'' In actuality, she was having a little difficulty adjusting to sharing her son.

While Jeff helped Joey into his pajamas, washed his face and brushed his teeth, Rebecca tidied his bedroom. There wasn't a lot to do, thanks to Betty. When it had just been the two of them, Rebecca had had trouble keeping up with the laundry and the toys and books, in addition to her job.

When the two men came out of the bathroom, Joey was giggling. "Mommy, Daddy said the new baby will be like my little brother or sister."

"Yes, I guess you could say that," she said slowly. She often wanted Joey to have a brother or sister, but that wasn't possible.

"That'll be okay, I guess. Will he be here in the morning? When I wake up?" Joey asked innocently.

"No, sweetie," Rebecca said, running her fingers through his unruly hair. "He'll be here in almost a year."

"Did I take that long?"

"Yes, you did," Rebecca said, avoiding Jeff's gaze. "Have you picked out a bedtime book for your daddy to read to you?"

"I want him to read my dinosaur book. And you come read some of it, too, Mommy. I want both of you to put me to bed."

Rebecca realized her son was getting a little spoiled, but she couldn't resist his request. She joined Joey and Jeff on the bed, the three of them cuddling around the book.

When they'd finished, she tucked in the sleepy little boy.

"That was nice, wasn't it, Mommy?" Joey asked.

"Yes, Joey, that was nice. Now, go to sleep." She kissed his cheek and pulled the covers up close.

Then Jeff leaned over and kissed Joey, too. "Good night, son."

The two adults backed out of the room, closing the door behind them.

"This is getting to be a regularity," Jeff said softly. "I like it."

"Joey enjoys having your attention." Rebecca moved toward the stairs.

"Was it like that when you found out about Joey? Were you happy?"

She turned and stared at him. "There was a momentary joy, but I had too much to worry about, Jeff. Being single and pregnant, without any money, is no picnic."

"I know that," Jeff said, acknowledging her words. "I just wanted to know that—that somewhere, sometime, you were happy."

"Yes, Jeff, there was happiness, but I had no one to share it with. I know, I know, I should've called you. But I didn't. I believed I was alone. After he was born, he was so—so beautiful, so perfect. Yes, there was joy."

"I don't mean to remind you of bad times, but I've missed so much of his young life. I sat down there listening to Will and Vivian, knowing that we'd never have a moment like that."

Jeff turned and paced the hallway. "I know we can't go back to change the past, but I wish we could."

Rebecca sighed and leaned against the wall. "Do you think I haven't thought that a jillion times? Do you think I wanted Joey and me to be alone? I don't want us to be alone now. But you're marrying Chelsea. I accept that. It would be helpful if you could accept the past, too."

"Yeah," Jeff said, his chin down. "I guess I'm not helping the situation any."

"No, you're not." She'd fought those battles when Joey was born. She'd wanted so much for her child. Now it appeared that Joey would receive at least some of what she'd wanted for him. She had to adjust to the fact that she wouldn't be a part of all Joey would receive. But she would accept it soon. It just took time to swallow the fact that Jeff wasn't going to be her partner in raising Joey.

"Let's not discuss the past, Jeff. It's gone. Let's deal with the present. I'm allowing you as much visitation as you want with Joey. And I think things are going well." She gave him a bright smile, one that hid tears and lonely nights.

"All right. We'll concentrate on the present…and the future. I'll see you at work tomorrow." With his hands in his pockets, Jeff went down the stairs.

Rebecca didn't follow.

Chapter Six

When Rebecca got to the office the next afternoon, Chelsea was waiting for her. Or at least that's what she said. She was busy talking to Bill when Rebecca came in.

Harriet, too, was waiting to talk to Rebecca. She'd learned Vivian's news and wanted to discuss it with her.

Jeff stood on the sidelines, watching the life of his office whirl around Rebecca. He was drawn to her, too, as he'd always been. But he remained still, waiting to see her reaction to Chelsea's plan.

"How is Vivian feeling?" Harriet asked.

"Very well, except for getting tired more frequently. She's taking naps, though."

"Oh, that's good. I'll have to take her to lunch to celebrate. This is so exciting."

"Yes, it is, Harriet. I'm sure she'd love to do lunch," Rebecca assured her, smiling.

"Rebecca, I have a great idea," Chelsea said almost before Rebecca had finished speaking.

"You do?" Rebecca asked politely, edging her way to the desk Harriet had assigned her.

Chelsea stayed right beside her. "Yes, it's a new thing for us to do with Joey. It's perfect."

"Okay, what is it?" Rebecca asked, putting her purse and books down on the desk.

"It's the Sesame Street Show on Ice. Jeff can get us very good tickets, maybe even front row. It will be wonderful." She was very enthusiastic.

"Why, that sounds like a fun thing to do. I'm sure Joey will enjoy it."

"I think we all will," Chelsea responded.

Jeff crossed his arms over his chest and grinned at Rebecca when her gaze met his.

"All?" Rebecca asked faintly.

"You, me, Bill and Jeff, of course, plus Joey. We mustn't forget Joey," she added with a laugh.

"But, Chelsea, surely you and Jeff can take Joey."

"Oh, no, not yet. You promised to teach me all about little boys. I don't know anything yet." Chelsea gave her a stubborn look that Jeff had seen before.

He suddenly noticed, too, that Chelsea was wearing jeans and a sweater, similar to what Rebecca had worn to the zoo. That was a change. A big change. Usually, Chelsea wore tailored slacks, silk shirts and jackets.

"But—" Rebecca began, and Jeff stepped forward.

"I think that's a good plan, Rebecca. And how hard can it be? We'll sit in air-conditioned seats and watch other people perform. It's not like we'd be camping out or going fishing or something."

He almost burst into laughter as he saw Chelsea's eyes light up. Would her next suggestion include some of those things? He wasn't sure what was going on, but he was willing to let it run its course. If nothing else, his fiancée would understand Joey and know how to deal with him more.

"That's right, Rebecca. And Bill said he'd buy us a hamburger beforehand." Chelsea exchanged a bright smile with Bill.

"Well, that's very nice of Bill, but surely it's not necessary," Rebecca responded, seemingly unsure of the invitation.

Bill stepped forward. "Don't be silly, Rebecca. It will be a treat for me. I'm so tired of eating alone." He pulled on a curl of Chelsea's blond hair. "It'll be fun to take all of you kids out to dinner. And hamburgers aren't that expensive."

Jeff touched Rebecca's arm. "You can tell Bill's willing. It will be fun, Rebecca. How about Friday night? Are you free then?"

Rebecca hesitated and Jeff's heart sped up. "What's wrong? Do you have a date then?"

"Of course not. Vivian was talking about having a celebration with their friends about their baby, and I—"

"Mrs. Greenfield is having a baby?" Chelsea asked.

"Yes, and—"

"But she's too old!" Chelsea exclaimed.

"No, she's not," Rebecca replied, for the first time

showing impatience. "She's only forty-three. I think it's wonderful."

"It is," Jeff agreed. "And we certainly don't want to take you away from Vivian's celebration. Why don't I call her? Then we can pick another night for our outing."

"That would be nice, Jeff," Rebecca agreed with a sweet smile. "I appreciate that."

Jeff went back into his office, glad things had worked out as they had. He called Vivian Greenfield. "Viv, this is Jeff Jacobs. We were trying to determine a date to take Joey to see Sesame Street on Ice. Rebecca was afraid this Friday might be your celebration for your baby."

"Oh, Jeff, thanks for checking with me. Yes, we were thinking about this Friday. Would that be a problem?"

"No, we can try to get tickets for Saturday night."

"Oh, good. And can you and your fiancée join us Friday night? We'd love to have you. It would be nice if someone were here that Rebecca knows."

"We'd be delighted. Do you mind if I bring my new partner? He doesn't know anyone in town and—"

"Oh, yes, that would be delightful. I'd love to meet him."

"Thanks, Vivian. His name is Bill Wallace. I think you'll like him."

"I'm sure I will. I'll look forward to introducing him to Will, too."

Jeff came out of his office to find Chelsea still

there, talking with Harriet and Bill. Rebecca appeared to be working. "Well, I talked to Vivian and they are having their celebration on Friday night, but we're all invited. So I think we should move Sesame Street to Saturday night."

"We're *all* invited?" Bill asked.

"Yeah. Vivian is looking forward to meeting you and introducing you to Will. You'll like him. He's a P.I."

"I don't want to intrude on a family event," Bill said, still hesitant.

"You won't be. You'll need to meet them, anyway, since they're our clients. They're genuinely nice people and it will be a good time. Right, Rebecca?"

She looked up, but it was obvious she'd been following what he'd said. "They really are, Bill. They took me and Joey in and they treat us like family."

"But I thought you were family," Chelsea said, frowning.

"We are, sort of. Vanessa and I are blood sisters, but they didn't have to be so generous."

"I bet they fell in love with Joey right away," Bill said.

"Yes, they did. And they spoil him rotten. But we were so alone until we moved down here, it's very good for Joey."

"And you," Jeff added softly.

Rebecca gave him a sharp look. "Well, yes, of course."

"Has Will found any of your other brothers or sisters?" Chelsea asked. "Are there others?"

"They've found our brother Jim. He's serving in the Middle East right now. We're hoping he'll get home on leave soon. Our brother Wally died over there. They haven't found David or my twin sister, Rachel."

"How strange to have a twin and not know where she is," Chelsea said. "Why did your parents give you all up for adoption?"

"They didn't," Jeff hurriedly said. "They were killed in a car crash and there were no other family members available, so the children all got split up and lost contact with one another."

"Oh, how sad." Chelsea looked appropriately subdued. "I just never thought about something like that happening."

"Life takes funny turns, Chelsea. You have to be strong to deal with what happens—look how Rebecca has managed." Jeff smiled at Rebecca even as he spoke.

"Well, if I'd been Rebecca, I would have given up. I certainly couldn't have managed on my own. That would have been too hard."

It was Bill who stepped forward to say, "You would have found a way to manage, Chelsea. I suspect you would have found a lot more strength in you than you'd imagined."

Chelsea gave him a solemn look. "I hope so."

FRIDAY NIGHT, REBECCA fixed Joey's collar and smoothed down his hair one more time. "Please be polite this evening. After a while, you can come upstairs and watch television, but we want to celebrate the new baby first.''

"Why do we celebrate the new baby when he's not even here yet?'' Joey asked. "He can't even have any cake.''

"No, he can't. But we celebrate him because he's a miracle.''

"What's a miracle?''

"It's something that happens in spite of everything.''

"Was I a miracle?'' Joey asked, staring at his mother.

"Yes, sweetie, you were. You're my special miracle.''

"And mine, too,'' a deep voice said over her shoulder.

"Oh, Jeff. I didn't know you were here. Is Chelsea with you?'' Rebecca hurriedly asked, hoping to hide her embarrassment.

"Yeah, she and Bill are downstairs with Vanessa. I came up to see if you two were ready.''

"Did you see the cake, Daddy? It has little baby shoes on it. Grandma Vivian said that's 'cause it's for the baby, but he doesn't get to eat any. Isn't that funny?''

"That's been fascinating him all afternoon,'' Rebecca explained.

"And driving you crazy?'' Jeff asked sympathetically.

"Yes. Joey, take your daddy's hand and go downstairs. I need to brush my hair and then I'll be down.''

"We could wait for you," Jeff suggested.

"You're as bad as Chelsea. You'll be fine." She hurried out the door to go to her room.

"I think Mommy's tired."

"You do? I guess I shouldn't have made her work today. I didn't think about that."

"She made me take a shower and change clothes and everything." There was a hint of a pout in those words that gave Jeff pause.

"You didn't give your mom a hard time, did you?"

Joey immediately shook his head no. "But I wanted to wear my jeans. Mommy said no."

"I figured you'd be in a suit, like me." Jeff led him to the stairs and started down them.

"I don't have a suit. Mommy said I should, but she said I grow too fast."

"Hmm, I need to discuss that with Mommy."

When they got downstairs, Jeff discovered the party had also become an opportunity for an announcement to all his clients and friends about Joey. Was that why Rebecca had lingered upstairs? Well, he guessed not. How could she have known that he was going to come upstairs to get them? When she finally did come down, Joey turned loose of his hand and immediately crossed the room to her side. Jeff followed.

"Are you feeling all right?" he asked.

"Yes, of course. Why?" she asked as she knelt down beside her son.

"Joey said you were tired."

"It was a busy day."

"I could've given you the afternoon off," he offered.

"It's all right," she said, rising. "Come on, Joey, let's go see if Betty and Peter need our help."

Which effectively excluded Jeff, he realized, as he watched them walk away.

"Where's Rebecca going?" Chelsea asked as she and Bill approached Jeff.

"I believe to the kitchen. Have you been introducing Bill around? I want him to meet any clients who are here."

"Yes, I have. Vanessa offered to do so, but I told her I'd manage," Chelsea assured him, looking proud of herself.

"I'm glad you met Vanessa," Jeff said to Bill. "I thought maybe we could double-date, if the two of you get along."

"I wouldn't mind," Bill assured him.

"I think she's seeing someone," Chelsea said at once.

"Really, who?"

"I don't know his name, but I'm sure they're pretty serious."

Rebecca came back into the room, crowded with people, without Joey. She joined her sister. Jeff immediately began moving in that direction and found Chelsea and Bill following him across the room.

"I just wanted to check on Joey."

"We wondered what happened to him, too," Chelsea assured him.

When the entourage arrived at Rebecca's side, she

introduced them to the group. As they were absorbed into the circle, new conversation forming, Jeff discovered Rebecca was no longer with them. Before he could ask her anything about Joey, she'd left their group and moved on to another one.

With a careful look at Bill and Chelsea, Jeff slipped from the group and went after Rebecca. "Are you trying to avoid me?" he asked in a whisper.

"Yes," she returned, much to his surprise.

"I was kidding," he protested.

"I wasn't. It's a little awkward to be introduced as the mother of your child but not your wife. It's easier if people connect the dots later, when I'm not around."

"I hadn't realized it would be embarrassing to you," he said slowly, thinking about what she'd said. "I guess that is more, uh, difficult for the mother than it is for the father."

"It's the double standard in American life. If a man produces a child, he's virile. If a woman produces a child without a man attached, she's easy." Rebecca had moved to the table and picked up a cup of punch.

"I'll knock the block off anyone who says such a thing," Jeff protested, horrified that he'd laid Rebecca open to such attitudes.

"It's not something you can do anything about. I'm not ashamed of Joey. But I don't want to encourage that opinion. When you and your fiancée are following me around, it arouses questions I don't want to answer."

"Maybe you should grab hold of Bill."

"Why?"

"He's a single guy. People would assume he was the new man in your life."

"And that would be good how?" she asked impatiently.

"I don't know. I just thought—I wasn't thinking."

"Hello, Rebecca, dear," a large woman said, interrupting their quiet conversation. "It's so good to see you again. And is this your young man?"

"No, Mrs. Bracken, this is the attorney I work for, Jeff Jacobs. Jeff, Mrs. Bracken is a longtime friend of Vivian's."

When Mrs. Bracken engaged him in conversation, calling over her husband to meet him, Rebecca slipped away.

This time Jeff didn't follow.

THE PARTY WAS ALMOST OVER and Vanessa and Rebecca were standing partially hidden by the French doors.

"I'm glad Mom doesn't have these kinds of parties very often. I feel like I've been at a family reunion," Vanessa said in a whisper.

"And has every one of them asked you what you think about having a little baby in the family?" Rebecca asked with a smile.

"Yes, of course. Just as they've asked you about Joey's daddy. I didn't realize how uncomfortable that would make it for you tonight, either."

"That's okay. Joey's up in bed and Chelsea has

taken hold of Jeff, so there are no more lifted eyebrows for me this evening.''

''Bill looks a little lost, though.''

''Yes, he does. Did you like him?''

''He's nice enough. Frankly, he seemed more interested in Chelsea than he did in anyone else.''

''Yes, I've been worried about that myself. We're all going to an ice show tomorrow night. Bill's buying us all dinner.''

''Why?'' Vanessa asked in surprise.

''I promised Chelsea I'd teach her about little boys. She said it was too early for her to take Joey out without me.''

''That's weird,'' Vanessa said, raising her eyebrows.

''I know. But if I don't teach her about little boys, she and Joey don't have a chance. She doesn't know much about being a kid, much less a boy. I think she must've been a miniature adult when she was Joey's age.''

''But she seems nice enough.''

''I know. It's not her fault. I haven't met her mother yet, but I get the feeling the woman was not motherly.''

Vanessa grinned. ''Not like Mom?''

''I don't think there could ever be a mother like Vivian. She's so loving.''

''Yes, she is. And that's why this baby is such a special gift to both of them.''

''I agree.''

Will called everyone's attention, lifting a punch

cup in a toast. "Here's to our baby, be it a boy or a girl. We feel blessed. And we thank you for sharing this evening with us."

"It's the baby who's blessed," Rebecca whispered.

"You're right. Just like Joey was blessed to have a mommy like you."

Rebecca hugged her sister, knowing how lucky she was to find this family.

The party began to break up. Chelsea looked around for Rebecca. "Oh, there you are. Tonight was fun. Vivian and Will really are nice people, aren't they?"

"Yes, they're the best," Rebecca agreed.

"Well, thank you for inviting us. We enjoyed it," she said, and leaned over and kissed Rebecca on the cheek, much to her surprise.

Bill was standing beside her and did the same thing, thanking her for the invitation. When Jeff stepped up after Bill, Rebecca immediately stuck out a hand. He took it in his and frowned at her. "What's wrong?"

"There's no need to thank me for your invitation. You know Vivian wanted to invite you."

"I know. And I enjoyed myself. I was glad I had a chance to introduce Joey to my friends. I hope it didn't cause you too much embarrassment."

"No. No, it didn't. And Joey liked it."

"He did? Did he say anything?"

"When I took him up to bed, he told me about you telling everyone he was your boy. He was very proud of that."

"Thank you, Rebecca, for telling me that. I appreciate it."

"Yes, well, good night."

"I'll see you tomorrow evening."

"Yes, of course."

Rebecca stood there, watching the threesome cross the room to tell Vivian and Will good-night. Then with a sigh, she slipped up the stairs. She'd had enough of polite society for one night.

Chapter Seven

Late Saturday afternoon, Rebecca came down the stairs with Joey, dressed in his jeans, much to his pleasure. "Now, Joey, your daddy will be here soon, so don't get dirty."

"I won't, Mommy, but I promised Peter I'd come say hi before I left."

"All right," Rebecca agreed, sighing as he ran down the hall. It was so hard to keep her son clean for any length of time.

"Rebecca, is that you?" Vivian called from the library.

"Yes, it is," Rebecca returned as she walked to the door of the library.

"Oh, don't you look nice. That rose color goes so well with your dark coloring. Just like Vanessa's."

"Yes, thank you."

"Come sit down. Are you waiting for Jeff?"

"And Chelsea and Bill."

"Oh. I didn't realize you were dating Bill. He seems so nice."

Rebecca hurried to make things clear before the

others arrived. "I'm not dating Bill, Vivian. He's just lonely and wants to be included. He said he hates to eat alone. And Chelsea feels better when the numbers are even. I—I think she gets a little jealous when Jeff spends a lot of his time with Joey."

"Oh, I see." Vivian looked at her husband, working at the desk. "Don't you, Will?"

"Yes, dear, I do." He grinned at Rebecca. "I thought maybe it took that many of you to keep Joey in line."

"Will Greenfield, you know very well that Joey's perfectly well behaved," Vivian protested.

"I think Will was teasing, Vivian," Rebecca said with a grin.

"He's always teasing me. But I kind of like it." Vivian looked fondly at her husband.

"It makes life a lot more fun," Rebecca said wistfully, "to share some laughter, you know. Jeff used to—" Much to Rebecca's relief, the doorbell rang before she could go too far down memory lane.

"That must be them. I'd better get Joey." She hurried into the kitchen and out the patio door where Peter could be found.

Betty showed Jeff, Chelsea and Bill into the library.

"Rebecca isn't here?" Jeff asked after looking around the room.

"Yes, she is," Will said. "She just went outside to get Joey."

"Won't he get dirty?" Chelsea asked, looking a little doubtful.

"No, I'm sure—" Vivian began only to be interrupted by Rebecca and Joey's entrance.

"Oh, there you are," Jeff said, walking forward and swinging Joey up into his arms for a hug. "How are you, son?"

"I'm fine, Daddy. I went to tell Peter hi."

"Good for you. Are you ready to go?"

"Yes. Mommy's ready, too."

"We wouldn't go without her," Jeff assured his son, looking across the room at Rebecca. "Ready?"

She nodded and led the way to the front door, telling Vivian and Will goodbye as she did so.

When they got to the car, Rebecca reached for the back door. So did Chelsea. "Don't you want to ride in front with Jeff?" Rebecca asked, surprised.

"I thought we'd do women and children in the back and men in the front," Chelsea said with a smile.

Rebecca said nothing else. The two men didn't seem to mind. Once they were in the car, it wasn't far to drive downtown to the American Airlines Center.

"I've never been here before," Rebecca said as they parked the car.

"You haven't?" Jeff asked. "This is where the pro basketball team plays their games. We'll have to come to a game sometime."

Rebecca didn't say anything.

Chelsea immediately chimed in. "Oh, yes, I'm sure Joey would like to see a basketball game, wouldn't you, Joey?"

"Sure," the young boy said. "What's a basketball game?"

Both men burst out laughing and Rebecca, too, couldn't resist a chuckle. Chelsea seemed a little flustered.

"You'll like it, Joey. It's a bunch of men playing with a round ball," Chelsea explained.

"Will they let me play?" Joey asked.

"No, you just watch them play."

"Oh."

"I'm sure he'd enjoy the game, Chelsea. He just hasn't seen the game before." Rebecca smiled at her son to reassure him.

"I thought everyone had heard of basketball games."

"We didn't have much time to spend watching sports, I'm afraid. After working all day, I'd pick up Joey from day care and we'd have time to fix dinner and clean up afterward, play a little, do some laundry and plan our next day before Joey had to go to bed. There just wasn't much spare time."

"Didn't you have anyone to help you?" Chelsea asked.

"No, I didn't," Rebecca said calmly.

Jeff protested Chelsea's question. "Really, Chelsea, do you think all single parents have maids?"

"I'm sorry, I guess I didn't think about it. I can't imagine having to do all of that alone."

"It's all right," Rebecca hurriedly assured her. "If you're not in that situation, you don't tend to think about these details."

"True," Bill chimed in. "I wouldn't think about laundry. Of course, he's such a little guy, he probably didn't have too much—"

Rebecca burst into laughter. "Oh, Bill, you have so much to learn. Children go through clean clothes like a hurricane. You practically have to do a load a day to keep up."

"And I've heard you have to buy a lot of things for a baby," Jeff added.

"Oh, yes," Rebecca agreed, rolling her eyes. "Just to go out for the evening, you feel like you have to pack enough to last a week. It's incredible."

"I admire you so much, Rebecca," Chelsea said slowly. "I don't know how you managed."

"When the time comes, you do what you have to do, Chelsea. You'd manage, just like I did." Rebecca smiled reassuringly.

"I don't know about that, but I hope so," Chelsea said.

"Come on. We need to find our seats," Bill said.

"I thought we were eating first," Rebecca said, confused.

"The show starts at six, so we thought we'd eat afterward."

Rebecca said nothing, but she knew that schedule wouldn't work on a regular basis for a four-year-old.

Joey walked beside her, holding her hand. Jeff fell back to take his other hand. Then he whispered to Rebecca, "We'll get him some snacks to hold him until dinner."

"Thank you. I didn't want to complain to Bill."

"Like me, he's inexperienced, but we're fast learners," Jeff assured her with a grin.

"I'm glad to hear it."

Two hours later, they'd watched the Sesame Street characters whirl around the ice, their movements based on several different stories. Joey had consumed cotton candy, popcorn and several sodas.

The last few minutes, he'd gotten strangely quiet.

"Joey, are you feeling all right?" she whispered as he crawled into her lap.

"No. I don't feel so good."

"Is it your tummy?"

"Uh-huh." He laid his head on her shoulder.

"I think we'd better go to the bathroom," she whispered in his ear, and tried to move him out of her lap so they could get up.

"What is it?" Jeff asked.

"Joey doesn't feel well. We're going to the bathroom."

"Wait just a minute and the show will be over. That way he doesn't have to miss the finale."

Rebecca didn't think the finale meant much to Joey. However, it was easier to do as Jeff said rather than argue with him. But she was wrong. They shouldn't have waited.

Joey spewed forth all those treats he'd eaten so eagerly, just barely missing Chelsea's skirt.

Chelsea screamed, drawing back into Bill.

Joey immediately began to cry, both from pain and embarrassment.

Rebecca got out tissues and mopped up Joey's face.

Fortunately, the vomit didn't get on anyone. "Jeff, would you alert a janitor, please?"

"Sure thing. Is he all right?"

"I'm sure he's feeling better now. He'll be all right," she assured Jeff, appreciating his worry.

After Jeff left, she turned to Bill and Chelsea. "If you want to climb over this mess and wait for us at the top of the stairs, that will be fine."

The two of them scrambled out of the row and up the stairs.

"I'm sorry, Mommy," Joey whispered.

"Sweetie, it's not your fault. Everything will be fine." She snuggled him up against her and rocked back and forth.

Jeff came running down the stairs. "Where are Bill and Chelsea?"

"They're waiting for us up top. It was a little unpleasant down here."

A man in a gray uniform came down the stairs, carrying a mop and bucket.

Jeff turned around to meet him. "I'll apologize again. We gave him too many treats on an empty stomach."

"Don't worry, sir. It happens all the time."

Jeff reached into his pocket and Rebecca saw him give the man some money. Then he turned and held out his arms for Joey.

"Jeff, he might get sick again and—"

"I wash just as well as you do. Come on, Joey, let me carry you to the car."

Joey seemed willing to make the transfer, and Rebecca prayed he wouldn't throw up on Jeff. It would completely destroy Joey.

Fortunately, they reached the car with no incidents.

Once they were settled in the back seat, Joey slumped against his mother, and the drive home was quick. When they arrived, Jeff got out and came around to get Joey to carry him into the house.

"Really, Jeff, I can carry him."

"You've been carrying him by yourself for too long." Jeff scooped Joey up, putting his head on his shoulder. "Bill, can you escort the ladies?"

Before Rebecca could protest, she found herself being guided to Vivian's front door, her elbow in Bill's firm grasp, just as he held Chelsea's with the other hand.

Betty had met Jeff at the door and immediately alerted Vivian that Joey was sick. By the time Rebecca followed them to Joey's room, she found both ladies hovering over him. She continued on to the bathroom and got the stomach medicine all mothers kept on hand. With a glass of water, she carried a spoon and the bottle to Joey's bedside.

"Open your mouth, Joey," Rebecca ordered softly. The little boy opened his mouth and his eyes.

"I'm going to put medicine in your mouth. I want you to swallow it all at once, okay? Then you can have some water."

Joey did as he was told. Then he fell back against his pillow, his eyes closed. Rebecca felt his cheeks and forehead. He wasn't running a fever. With relief, Rebecca began undressing him.

"Don't we need to call a doctor?" Jeff asked, still hovering over the bed.

"No. He's not running any fever. He's asleep now. I don't think he'll wake up until the morning." Rebecca pulled off each little tennis shoe and put them side by side at the end of the bed. She folded Joey's jeans. Then she pulled the covers over him.

"Thanks for helping, Jeff. I hope he didn't ruin the evening for you."

"But what about dinner?" Jeff asked, recognizing a dismissal when he heard one.

Betty and Vivian stared at him. "Good heavens, you haven't eaten yet?" Vivian asked in surprise.

"No. We were going to eat after the show."

"I can fix something—"

Jeff stopped Betty's offer. "No, we're not going to ask you to dirty your kitchen again. But if Joey's going to sleep, can't you come out for dinner?" he asked Rebecca.

"Oh, no, he might wake up and call for me. I'd better stay here," she quickly said.

"Now, Rebecca, there's no need for that," Betty assured her. "I was going to watch a movie. I can watch in the room next door and be able to hear Joey if he calls. And don't you dare say you're a better mother than me."

"Of course not, Betty." What could Rebecca say?

"So you go off for dinner with your friends and I'll keep an eye on young Joey."

"I think that's a good idea, Rebecca. You need to

relax a little. You never go out.'' Vivian nodded as she folded her arms in determination.

''But, Vivian—'' Rebecca began, but Vivian told her again she should go.

Jeff took her arm. ''All the votes have been cast, young lady, and you are the lucky winner of a free dinner and night out. Come on.'' Over her shoulder he mouthed the words ''Thank you'' to Vivian and Betty.

They met the other two downstairs and again got into the car, women in the back seat.

''I'm so glad you could come,'' Chelsea said. ''Is Joey all right?''

''He will be. All those snacks on an empty stomach weren't a good idea. He usually eats dinner by six-thirty,'' she explained.

''Oh, I need to remember that,'' Chelsea said, frowning.

Bill looked at her over his shoulder. ''I don't think you'll forget that experience very quickly, Chelsea. You must've jumped a foot or two. I thought you were going to climb on top of me.'' His grin told all of them he wouldn't have minded.

''I was surprised,'' Chelsea protested, her cheeks red.

''Of course you were,'' Rebecca agreed, sending a reproving look toward Bill's grin.

''Well, I should be the one apologizing,'' Bill said. ''I didn't realize Joey ate that early.''

''I'm afraid so. And it helps if he stays on a regular schedule, which makes things difficult some days.''

"Maybe I understand now why my friends' lives changed so dramatically when they had a baby." Bill was now frowning as much as Chelsea.

"Yes, and if you add to that lack of sleep, for at least the first year, and the cost of baby-sitters as well as the difficulty of finding a good one, you have many reasons they're not interested in going out on the town anymore," Rebecca said with a smile.

"Makes me think having a baby is no light decision," Bill said. "I'd always figured on a couple of rug rats, but I didn't think it would change my life that much."

Rebecca just laughed.

"Well, it's easier if there are two of you, isn't it?" Chelsea asked.

Rebecca shrugged. "I guess it would be. But I've heard of some husbands who don't participate in raising their children. They leave it all to their wives."

"Ooh, I'd hate that," Chelsea said. "I'd divorce him."

"And then you'd be left on your own."

"But he'd have to pay me child support."

"Not all of them do. And the law is slow in catching up to them. I learned about that in law school," Jeff added.

"That's not fair," Chelsea protested.

"No, it's not, but life isn't fair. And you can't take a baby to the return department and tell them you want your money back," Rebecca pointed out.

"No, I guess not. Joey's not my child, but already, with as little time as I've spent with him, I couldn't give him up,'' Chelsea said, winning Rebecca's approval.

"Good for you," she said with a big smile.

Jeff gave his fiancée an appreciative smile in the rearview mirror. "I'm glad to hear that, Chelsea."

That was a bittersweet moment for Rebecca. She had convinced Joey's future stepmother that her son was important, which earned Chelsea Jeff's approval.

Bill cleared his throat. "Uh, since Joey's not dining with us, I wondered if maybe you'd like to upgrade a little from hamburgers. I know a good steak place. It's usually crowded, but since it's almost nine, maybe they could work us in."

"Oh, good," Chelsea said. "I wasn't in the mood for a hamburger."

Bill laughed. "Somehow I'm not surprised. You always prefer the expensive."

"It's the way she was raised," Jeff added with a grin.

"I think Chelsea has the right approach," Rebecca said staunchly. "You go for the best and then adjust as necessary."

"Our ladies are in agreement," Bill said. "We're in trouble."

THEY LINGERED OVER THEIR meal. Bill offered drinks, but no one took him up on his offer. Life was too perfect as it was. They enjoyed a steak dinner, the meat perfectly cooked, the baked potato just right, and a dinner salad with the right blend of ingredients.

"That was perfect," Rebecca said with a sigh. "I like your choice of restaurant, Bill."

"Hey, I might have chosen this restaurant," Jeff protested.

"And if you had, I would've complimented you. But Bill chose the restaurant for us, so I complimented him," Rebecca said.

"I accept the compliment. I just stumbled upon it by accident," he said.

"Do you eat out a lot?" Chelsea asked.

"Yeah. After working all day, I'm not much in the mood to cook. Besides, I'm not very good at it."

"That must get expensive," Chelsea said with a frown.

The two men stared at each other.

"Should we take her temperature?" Bill asked.

"Probably. She must be sick to think such a thing," Jeff returned.

Chelsea protested, her cheeks bright red.

"Don't let them bother you, Chelsea," Rebecca said softly.

"I just meant—"

"We know what you meant," Bill said, relaxing in his chair. "And you're right. But if I'm no good in the kitchen, my options are limited."

"I was just going to point out that it would be more cost-effective to marry and have a wife who cooks."

"Some wives work, too," Rebecca pointed out.

"But you said you fixed dinner after working all day," Chelsea replied.

"I did for two reasons. I didn't have enough money

to eat out often, and I cooked because it wouldn't be good for Joey's diet to eat out all the time.''

"It's not good for mine, either," Bill said. "I'm getting fat."

The other three laughed since Bill's frame was as slender as ever.

The waiter brought back the receipt from Bill's credit card. As he signed it, the ladies gathered their purses to leave.

"This has been so nice," Chelsea said. "I even enjoyed the conversation."

"Well, you should have," Jeff agreed. "We covered every subject in the book. You had to stay alert to keep up."

"But it was fun and so refreshing to have some adult companionship. Joey's line of conversation may be sweet," Rebecca said, "but it's not very intellectual yet or mind-stimulating."

"Not even when he wants to know what certain words mean?" Jeff asked, raising an eyebrow.

Rebecca blushed. "He's asked about a couple of those words. The next time he does, I'll tell him to ask his father."

"They start asking difficult questions that young?" Chelsea asked with a gasp. "I thought that wouldn't happen until maybe middle school."

"Oh, no," Rebecca said with a sigh. "I've been told most of those questions come by the fourth grade. They hear other children talking. Our children get an incredible education on the playground or school bus. Just not the education we want for them."

"Maybe we should consider private school," Jeff said.

"Then they get the same information, only with an attitude," Chelsea said. "Now that I think about it, I remember things I heard on the playground. But I knew better than to ask my mother what they meant."

Bill stood and they began walking out. "Who did you ask, then?" Bill asked, curious.

"My girlfriends."

"But they may not have known the truth. They might have been making up something. You would have never known the difference." Bill sounded horrified, as if he always got the correct answer to his embarrassing questions.

"You're right, they didn't know," Chelsea responded with a laugh. "I remember one—oh, no, I can't say that!" she exclaimed, her cheeks bright red.

"Can't say what? Now you have to say it." Bill said.

"Never mind. I can assure you I know what it is now." Chelsea ducked into the back seat before Bill could ask any more questions.

"Don't look at me," Rebecca quickly warned the two men. "I think I'm too young to know what Chelsea is talking about."

"Fine talk for a woman who has given birth. Definitely tell Joey to ask me anything anytime," Jeff advised, a grin on his face.

Chapter Eight

On Monday, when Rebecca reached the office to work, she checked with Harriet to see if Jeff had a full slate of appointments.

"Why, no, dear, he's free this afternoon. Mondays aren't busy days. Do you need to talk to him?"

"Yes, I think I do." Rebecca had done a lot of thinking after their Saturday evening adventures. As much as she hated to admit it, both Jeff and Chelsea knew enough about Joey to take him out alone now, without her.

It seemed to Rebecca that there was something unnatural about the foursome that resulted when she and Bill came along. She'd decided that for her own protection, she'd better bow out of any future evenings like Saturday.

Rebecca actually thought Chelsea was genuinely nice and intelligent, which didn't make Rebecca find the foursome any easier. She could admit to herself that she was still in love with Jeff. And the more time she spent with him in intimate settings, even with the other two along, made it harder for her to deal with his future marriage to Chelsea.

"Rebecca? Jeff said he could see you now." Harriet stood there smiling at her, and Rebecca had to pull herself together, even though she felt like bursting into tears.

"Oh, thank you, Harriet. I won't take up much of his time."

Harriet just nodded and went back to work. She was such a dear woman, never interfering in others' business.

Rebecca stepped into the office and closed the door behind her before she faced Jeff. He was sitting behind his desk, and she would prefer that he kept it between them.

"Have a seat, Becca. What's up?"

"Nothing, really. I just wanted to tell you that I don't think I need to accompany Joey every time you want to take him out anymore. Both you and Chelsea are very good with him and could handle him on your own."

Instead of responding to her statement, he stood and came around the desk. "You aren't even going to take a seat to have this conversation?"

"I don't want to take up too much of your time," Rebecca said, backing toward the door.

"Come on, Becca, I think we need to talk about what you just said."

"I don't think so," she contradicted him. "I need to get back to work."

"You make me sound like a slave driver. By the way, I'm giving you a raise."

Those words stopped her progression to the door. "What? Why are you doing that?"

"Because you're a hard worker. Besides, you spent four years paying for everything yourself. I owe you. I'm also setting up a college fund for Joey so that if anything happens to me, that part of his life will be taken care of. Bill is going to be the trustee."

"The—the college fund is nice, and Bill will do well as the trustee, I'm sure. That's very nice, but you don't owe me anything, Jeff."

"Yes, I do. That's why we need to talk. I'm going to start child support payments at once. We need to talk about the amount."

"No! I—I didn't ask for child support money." Her heart was beating too rapidly, and she found difficulty drawing a breath.

He took her arm and led her to one of the chairs in front of his desk. He took the other one. "I know you didn't ask for it, but I'm going to pay it, anyway. I thought a flat settlement for the past four years and then a monthly stipend of two thousand dollars would be fair."

The splits he mentioned took her breath away. "N-no! Absolutely not. You owe me nothing for those four years. You didn't even know Joey existed. That wouldn't be fair. And—and that's too much for each month."

"I think you should have enough so that if you need a place of your own, you could afford it." He reached out and took her hand in his. "If you don't, then you can use the money for Joey's expenses and put the rest of the money in savings for another time."

"Jeff, I just came in to tell you the foursome wouldn't be necessary anymore. That's all. I don't want to talk about—about money. I'm grateful you want to spend time with Joey. That's all I ever wanted for him."

"I know, sweetheart, but you've got to think about your and Joey's future."

"I have thought about it. That's all I ever think about. I'm going to have my teaching certificate in three more semesters. Then I'll earn a good salary and have more time to spend with Joey."

"And that's a good plan. But if you save your child support, you may be able to buy your own place by then. That would be nice, wouldn't it?"

She got up from the chair and backed away from him. "I have to go to work." Before he could stop her, she opened the door and escaped back into Harriet's company.

"My heavens, child, what's wrong? Did Jeff give you bad news?" Harriet immediately asked. "You're so pale. You'd better sit down at once."

"N-no, Harriet, I'm fine, really," Rebecca said, moving toward her own desk. "I just need to start work."

Harriet's eyes went past Rebecca, and Rebecca whirled around to discover Jeff had come to his office door. He nodded to Harriet, and she immediately began showing Rebecca her work for the day.

Jeff went back into his office and picked up the phone. When his caller answered, he said, "Will, I need to talk to you about something. I'm trying to arrange things financially with Rebecca, and she won't discuss it at all. Could I come to your office and show you what I want to do, so you could tell me if I'm being fair to Rebecca? And help me convince her to accept what I'm offering?"

"I'll be glad to talk to you about it, Jeff, of course. You understand that I don't have legal guardianship for Rebecca. She's completely independent."

"Don't I know it. But I want to protect her and Joey from—from whatever could go wrong in their lives. Could I come in half an hour?"

"Of course. We'll try to work out something Rebecca could accept."

"Thanks, Will. I'll see you in a little while."

Jeff hung up the phone and stared at the painting on the wall. He wanted to be there for Rebecca and Joey. He gave a disparaging laugh. What he really wanted was to marry Rebecca, but he'd promised to marry Chelsea, and she didn't deserve to be dumped now.

His only hope was the foursome Rebecca had just tried to end. It seemed to him that his fiancée was responding to Bill more than she did to him. And he knew Bill was attracted to Chelsea, too. He was his friend and would never try to break up his engagement. But he wanted Chelsea.

So it was up to Jeff to continue these foursomes until whatever might happen, happened. He'd already bought tickets to the opening night of the basketball season for their local pro team. He'd bought five tickets, planning to use the excuse of taking Joey to the basketball game.

He felt sure he could convince Rebecca to come so he didn't waste his money on a ticket for her that she wouldn't use. But what else could he find for the five of them to do without Rebecca catching on?

His phone rang. "Jacobs."

"Jeff, I have a wonderful idea," Chelsea announced without any preliminaries. "I think we should take Joey to Six Flags before they close for the season. I think this Saturday is the last day. It would be so much fun for the five of us."

"I think you're right, Chelsea. I'll ask Bill. Why don't you call Rebecca and check with her."

"Isn't she at work with you?" Chelsea asked, sounding confused.

"Yes. You see, she's decided we are ready to take Joey without her, which is a compliment to you, darling, but I think it would be nice if she came with us to Six Flags. After all, it would be an all-day event, and some of the rides are rather scary."

"Oh, I see. Okay. I'll call her."

"Good. Don't take no for an answer."

"I won't."

Jeff immediately went to Bill's office as soon as he'd hung up the phone. "Bill, do you think you could stand another outing with Joey?"

"Of course I could. He's a fine boy, Jeff. You should be proud."

"I am. But his throwing up might make you a little hesitant about wanting to accompany us anymore," Jeff said with a laugh.

"As long as I don't have to clean up after him, I'm happy to go along."

"Well, Chelsea has suggested that we all go to Six Flags this Saturday. It's the last weekend they're open until next spring."

"Chelsea's just full of good ideas, isn't she?" Bill asked with a laugh. "That sounds like fun."

"Okay, she's checking with Rebecca now. I'm on my way to an appointment, but one of us will let you know the details. I'll be back later this afternoon."

He hurried out of the office with a whispered goodbye to Harriet, not wanting Rebecca to see him leave. He knew she was on the phone with Chelsea, and she didn't seem happy about what was being said. He was pretty sure he could count on Chelsea to convince her, though.

Was he being fair to Chelsea? He was using her enthusiasm and reluctance to deal with Joey on her own. But he thought he was doing the right thing. Better for them to be sure their marriage would work before they both made a terrible mistake.

REBECCA GOT OFF THE PHONE with Chelsea and stood to go back to Jeff's office.

"Are you looking for Jeff? He's gone out, Rebecca. He had an appointment."

"Oh. I didn't see him leave. When will he be back?"

"I'm not sure. Bill is here if you need to talk to him."

"No, thank you, Harriet. I'll just get started on the filing." Rebecca could think of nothing she wanted to say to Bill. According to Chelsea, Jeff knew of her plans and had promised to tell Bill.

So Jeff had completely ignored her determination to avoid any foursome in the future. Why? Didn't he know how hard it was for her to see him escorting Chelsea? She had to admit, of course, that he didn't appear to do much escorting since he was doting over her and Joey most of the time.

Poor Chelsea. Rebecca thought she would be glad to avoid the foursomes, but here she was trying to set up another one. And it did sound like fun, of course. Joey would love Six Flags, she was sure.

She tried to put it out of her mind. She had work to do. Harriet had left her a lot of filing. If Jeff was giving her a raise, she'd better earn it.

JEFF SPENT A SATISFYING hour with Will. He liked the man, and he was able to be honest with him. As honest as he could be. "Are you and Vivian happy having Rebecca and Joey there with you? Because I can pay for a place for them to live on their own."

"Vivian would kill me if I aided you in removing one of her chicks from the nest. Truthfully, Jeff, we love having them there. It means a lot to Vanessa to have her sister there, to get to know her better. And Joey has stolen all of our hearts.''

"But with you having a child of your own, things may get a little more complicated.'' Jeff watched him carefully, looking for any sign that Rebecca and Joey were burdens to him.

Will laughed. "Do you really think Betty couldn't handle a dozen children and still be happy? It's not like it's Vivian and me doing all the work."

"Betty is good with Joey and she's terrific in the kitchen. I have a lady who cleans my house regularly, but she doesn't do much cooking."

"Well, we're fine, but I promise to let you know if I think it would be better for Rebecca and Joey to be out on their own. But I really don't like the idea. There are too many bad guys looking for lonely women to target."

"I know. And I appreciate the protection you provide them."

"Happy to do it," Will assured him.

"Here's what I had in mind for child support," Jeff said, showing Will a piece of paper where he'd written out his intentions.

Will studied the figures. Then he looked at Jeff. "These are very generous numbers."

"Joey is my child, and Rebecca is his mother because I was careless with her. She—she deserves better than just money, but it's all I can offer in my present situation."

"I see. Well, she should have no complaints with this much money."

"The problem will be getting her to agree to it. She says I don't owe her anything, and she doesn't want me to pay child support."

"Hmm. Well, I'll try to talk to her, but it might be better handled by Vivian. She'll explain why Rebecca should accept this amount, for Joey's sake, of course."

"I'd appreciate that, Will. Were you able to offer any assistance to Dr. Janvers?" he asked, referring to the man he'd sent to Will.

"Yes, I was. In fact, I've done several jobs for him since you referred him. I appreciate the business, Jeff."

"Hey, you're the closet thing to family, other than Joey, that I have. Any business I can send your way, I'm more than happy to do so. How are your searches for the other siblings coming along?"

"David and Rachel, if those are the names they go by, have proved elusive. I haven't discovered the name of their adopted parents. They haven't signed any of the lists of children seeking their real families. I've tracked down some Rachels and Davids but they weren't adopted. But I'll keep looking. I promised Vivian I'd find them."

"It would mean a lot to Rebecca to find her twin. She enjoys Vanessa a lot, I think, but I've always heard twins were special."

"Yes, me, too. Hopefully, I'll find them soon."

Jeff stood and held out his hand. "I appreciate your help on this. Let me know if there's ever anything I can do for you."

"If you run across any Rachels or Davids that look like Vanessa and Rebecca, let me know," Will said with a laugh.

"You got it," Jeff promised.

He left, saying goodbye to Carrie, Will's assistant. He thought he'd met her before, but he wasn't sure.

On the way out, he pulled out his cell phone and dialed Chelsea's number. "Chelsea? It's Jeff. Did you talk to Rebecca?"

"Yes. She's very stubborn, but I convinced her to go. Did you talk to Bill?"

"Yeah, he's fine with it. So we're set for Saturday. What time shall I pick you up?"

"I think we should get there about ten. So you should pick me up at nine, and Rebecca and Joey at nine-fifteen. Oh, and you should get Bill before you pick me up, too."

"Right. So I'll see you Saturday."

"Well, you could call me sometime before Saturday."

"Oh, yeah," he agreed with a laugh. "I'll do that."

But his mind was on Rebecca and his son. Joey was becoming almost the most important person in his world. Well, maybe second. That didn't leave a place for Chelsea until number three. That wasn't the way things should be. Not for his fiancée. But it was the way things were.

He had to be patient.

AFTER DINNER THAT EVENING, Will quietly asked if he and Vivian could talk to Rebecca after she put Joey to bed.

"Yes, of course," she immediately agreed, her mind filling with worry about what might be wrong.

"Did you do something?" Vanessa whispered as she walked beside her sister.

"Not that I know of. Do you think they're going to ask me to leave?"

"Of course not. Mom wouldn't do that for any reason, but certainly not without discussing it with me." Vanessa sighed. "Maybe I should go with you."

"To protect me?" Rebecca asked with a grin. "I'm the big sister, remember?"

"I remember," Vanessa said, hugging Rebecca. "But I'll go with you, anyway, unless you don't want me to."

"I'd love for you to go with me. I'll admit to being a little worried."

"Worried about what, Mommy?" Joey asked. He was holding Rebecca's hand and had listened to their conversation.

"Oh, nothing, sweetie. Mommy's just being silly. Did I tell you about the latest thing your daddy and Chelsea have planned for you?"

"What?"

"He wants us to go to Six Flags on Saturday."

"What's that?"

Vanessa answered his question. "Six Flags is a lot of fun. They have lots of rides and things to do. There are games and prizes, too."

"That sounds like fun. I won't get sick this time, Mommy," Joey promised solemnly.

"Of course not. It wasn't your fault you got sick last time. If it was anyone's fault, it was mine, sweetie. Don't worry about it."

"Did Daddy get angry about it?" Joey asked.

Rebecca felt she'd failed as a mother when she realized her son must've been worrying about having disappointed his father.

"Not at all. He wouldn't want to take us to the Six Flags amusement park if he was upset about it or if he was worried about it happening again, Joey. I promise."

"Oh, good."

Rebecca exchanged a look with Vanessa. Her sister, too, had realized how worried Joey was.

"Hey, Joey, want some of my bubble bath in your tub tonight? We could build castles out of soap bubbles," she suggested.

"Could we, Mommy?" Joey eagerly asked.

"Yes, I think that would be all right. But we need to put you in the bath at once if you're going to play awhile. You need to go to bed at eight."

"Okay. Let's go, Vanessa," Joey immediately agreed, grabbing his aunt's hand.

"All right, go with Vanessa. I'll be there in a moment."

Rebecca stood there, watching her son skip down the hall. She'd intended to fight the trip to the amusement park, but she now knew she couldn't. Joey needed to believe his father didn't hold any resentment toward him because he got sick in front of everyone.

Rebecca went to her room and picked up the phone. She had to look up Jeff's number, but she found it easily enough. When his deep voice answered, she panicked and couldn't say anything.

"Hello? Is anyone there?"

"Yes, it's me, I mean, it's Rebecca."

"Hello, sweetheart, is everything okay?"

"Yes, but don't call me that."

He didn't question her words. "Sorry, it just comes out naturally."

"I called because I discovered Joey's been worried all week that you were upset with him because he got sick."

"Of course I wasn't. It was my fault more than his."

"And I blame myself. But I wanted you to know that he was worried. I—I told him you wouldn't want to take him to Six Flags if you were upset."

"I think that's true."

"That's why I'm agreeing to go on Saturday. I wanted you to know that I haven't changed my mind about—about our foursomes. But for Joey's sake, I can't protest this last outing."

"I understand. Uh, I've already purchased tickets for another outing. I bought them Monday morning, before you said anything. I'm hoping you'll make that outing an exception, too."

"Where is it?"

"It's the basketball game. The opening game of the

season is special and I know someone in the box office, so I was able to persuade him to get us courtside seats. It will be very exciting."

Rebecca held her breath. Finally, she blew out the hot air. "I guess I could go along with that, since you've already bought the tickets."

"Thanks, Becca. I think Joey will enjoy it."

"I hope so. Thank you, Jeff, for—for taking him into your heart."

"It wasn't hard, honey. He's very important to me. As you are, as his mother. I'm going to take care of both of you."

"No! Just Joey."

"You haven't talked to Will yet?"

"No," Rebecca said slowly, suspicious. "Why would you ask that?"

"Nothing, it doesn't matter. We'll work things out, okay?"

"Okay. Good night."

"Good night, sweetheart."

She didn't remind him again not to call her that. She just hung up the phone, reminding herself that he didn't have the right to call her that, even if it did fill her with love for him.

Chapter Nine

After Joey was tucked in, the two ladies headed back down to the library, where Will and Vivian were waiting.

When Vanessa entered with Rebecca, she immediately said, "I'm here to support Rebecca and she's okay with that."

Will raised one eyebrow. "You thought we were going to browbeat Rebecca?"

"We didn't know why you wanted to talk to her. She was nervous and I wanted to support her," Vanessa said again, challenging her stepfather with the lift of her chin.

"She's definitely got the Barlow chin," he said to his wife.

"Of course we don't mind if you're here, Vanessa, as long as Rebecca doesn't mind. And, my dear Rebecca, we didn't ask you to come talk to us because you did something bad. Jeff wanted Will to talk to you about his financial arrangements. He said you didn't want to accept what he offered."

Vanessa turned to stare at her sister. "Why not?"

"I didn't even tell him about Joey until he was almost four years old, Vanessa. It hardly seems fair that he wants to give me money for that time period. Besides, I'm doing all right, thanks to your parents, so why should I take his money?"

"He wants to provide for the two of you, for your future," Will said quietly.

"Dear," Vivian began, "I know you're doing fine right now, but no one knows what twists and turns fate will bring us. If you don't need his money now, have him put it in a trust fund for you or Joey. If after Joey reaches a certain age you don't need the money, you can give it back to him."

Rebecca nibbled on her bottom lip. Finally, she raised her head. "I could do that. We could put it in a trust for Joey. But Jeff's already started a college fund for him."

"How about I call Jeff tomorrow and we hammer out a trust fund agreement? He can draw up the papers and have you sign them when you go into work," Will suggested.

"Will you encourage him to reduce the numbers he originally offered this morning?" Rebecca asked.

"I'll certainly tell him that's what you'd like."

"Well, while you're all here, I'd like to ask something that's been on my mind. Will, are you and Vivian sure you don't mind Joey and me staying here?"

"Of course we're sure," Vivian immediately answered, without pause. "You're family, and we enjoy having you here."

"But with the baby coming—"

"We'll need you even more," Will assured her.

"You're the only one in the house who has been through delivery. You'll be a great support for Vivian. And you'll provide an extra set of hands and be another baby-sitter in the house."

Her eyes watering, Rebecca smiled. "You two are such wonderful people. I can't thank you enough for what you give to me and Joey. He's just blossomed since he's been surrounded by family."

"He's a wonderful little boy," Vivian assured her. "We only hope ours is as good."

"He or she will be, Vivian, because they'll be surrounded by such a loving family."

"Well, now that we've all patted one another on the backs, I think it's time we disband for an early night," Will said. "Mothers-to-be need lots of rest."

They all went up the stairs together, happily ending another evening.

REBECCA AVOIDED JEFF as much as possible for the rest of the week. She tried to be sure she was busy at all times, especially when she knew he was in the office. Will had talked to Jeff and brought home papers for her to sign. Since the money didn't matter to her and she trusted Will, she didn't bother to read them. Will assured her that the money would go straight into a fund, and she could return it to Jeff when Joey was an adult if she chose to do so.

She didn't want his money when he couldn't give her what she really wanted. His love.

Saturday was a cool fall day at the end of September. She dressed herself and her son appropriately and made sure Joey ate a good breakfast. It took work. He jumped down from his seat every time he heard a car go by.

"Joey," she called for the fifth time, "come back and finish your breakfast."

"But—"

"Now!" She seldom used that tone, but she was running out of patience.

Joey slid back into his chair. "I bet this trip is my birthday present. It's almost my birthday, isn't it?"

Since Joey had had his mom mark off each day on the calendar before October 2, which was circled in red, Joey knew it was only five days until his birthday.

"Don't you remember? We're taking cupcakes to school for your birthday, Joey." Rebecca felt badly that she wasn't giving her son a birthday party. He'd never had one. But she didn't want to add to Betty's chores or bring the disruption of a children's party to Vivian's quiet home.

"How many days away is it?" Betty asked as she took dishes to the sink.

Joey held up four fingers because that's the age he was going to turn. "My birthday is October 2."

"It is? No one told me about that."

Rebecca smiled at warmhearted Betty. "I've been trying to keep him quiet about it. But we will be invading your kitchen to bake cupcakes for his class on Wednesday night."

"Aren't you going to have a birthday party?" Betty asked.

"Oh, those are kind of noisy. We'd have to invite the entire class and there's eighteen kids in it."

"Plus Daddy, Chelsea and Bill. They're my friends, too," Joey announced. "And you and Peter and Grandpa Will and Grandma Vivian and Aunt Vanessa."

"Mercy, you have a big party list, young man."

Joey gave her a big grin. "I do, don't I? I'm a lucky boy."

Rebecca kissed his forehead. "Yes, you are. Go upstairs and brush your teeth and we'll be ready to go."

As soon as Joey left the room, Betty asked, "Are you sending out the invitations on Monday?"

"The invitations for what?"

"Joey's party. We can have it here. I'll bake him a super birthday cake and get ice cream. We can feed them all hot dogs before they eat ice cream and cake. We'll find some games to play and you can buy prizes, just little things, you know. We can invite the mothers, too, if they want to come. I could fix some chicken salad sandwiches for them, just in case they're not fond of hot dogs."

"Betty, that's too much trouble for you and it's only five days away. I thought I'd just take Joey to McDonald's for his birthday."

"And rob us of our chance to celebrate Joey's birthday? I'll talk to Miz Vivian while you're gone today. I'm sure she'll agree."

"But she needs to rest more these days. I don't want her to overdo anything and get tired."

"I can handle a birthday party with one hand behind my back, young lady."

The doorbell rang, and Betty left the kitchen before Rebecca could say anything. She gathered the dishes left from their breakfast and took them to the sink. She heard Joey's running footsteps in the hallway and stepped out there in time to remind him that he should not run in the house.

"But Daddy's here, Mommy. I saw his car out of the window."

Betty led Jeff into the hallway, and Joey ran to his father, arms outstretched. Jeff swung him up into his arms, as he always did. "Are you ready, son?"

Joey beamed. "Yes, Daddy. Is this my birthday present?"

"Your birthday present? No, this is just for fun. I'll get you a birthday present, something you can unwrap."

"Oh, goody," Joey squealed, and hugged his father's neck again.

Betty patted Rebecca's shoulder. "Don't you worry none about the party. I'll take care of everything." Then she went back into the kitchen.

Rebecca was left standing with her mouth open.

"What's wrong, Becca?"

Rebecca looked from Jeff's concerned face to Joey's big smile and said, "I'll have to tell you later."

"Bill and Chelsea are waiting in the car. Are you ready?"

"I'll just get my purse."

"Why don't you leave it? That way you can't lose it on the rides."

"But I'll need it."

"For what? I've got enough money for us today."

"But I might want to buy something."

"So, I'll buy it and you can pay me back."

She glared at him, but he continued to smile at her. "Let me get some tissues in case we have an emergency," she muttered. She returned several minutes later and nodded that she was ready to go. She'd stuck a ten-dollar bill into her pocket along with a couple of tissues.

Chelsea was waiting in the back seat. Joey actually gave her a hug. When Bill complained he didn't get a hug, Joey stood in the back seat and hugged Bill's neck, too. Then Rebecca buckled him in.

It was a forty-five-minute drive and Joey got impatient, wanting to know if they were there yet several times, until Rebecca told him he couldn't ask that question again. He sagged against her and actually fell asleep for the last twenty minutes.

When Jeff saw that Joey was asleep, he asked quietly, "What do you have planned for his birthday?"

"When's his birthday?" Bill asked.

"Next Thursday, the second."

Everyone turned to look at Rebecca.

Finally Chelsea said, "And you didn't tell us?"

"I thought I'd take him to McDonald's for his birthday. Now, of course, that's all changed."

"What's changed?" Jeff asked.

"Betty told me this morning that she would organize a birthday party for him and all the kids in his class and the mothers, too. Joey immediately told her you all would have to be invited, too, and Peter, Will, Vivian and Vanessa."

"And you agreed?" Jeff asked.

"I didn't have a choice. Betty was kind of hurt that I hadn't mentioned it before."

"We are, too," Bill complained. "It'll take some time to pick out a good present."

"Please, don't spend a lot on him. I don't want him to get too spoiled."

They all assured her they wouldn't, but Rebecca didn't believe them. She hugged her little boy closer to her, thinking what a lucky child he was. Her own birthdays hadn't been treated as special days. She'd never had a birthday party.

When they drove into the parking lot, she awakened Joey. "Joey, it's time to wake up. We're here."

One would've thought she'd clicked on a switch. From a sleeping child, Joey turned into an excitable boy in no time at all. "Where? Where is it, Daddy? I can't see it."

Jeff picked up Joey and pointed through the trees. "It's over behind those walls. We'll just get on this little train—" he waved down a tram that gave rides to the front "—and we'll be there in no time." At that, the five of them boarded the train.

Rebecca suddenly noticed that because she wanted to stay close to Joey, and that was the only reason, she assured herself, she was seated with Joey and Jeff, which left Bill and Chelsea to sit together.

"I should change seats with Chelsea," she whispered, and started to move. Jeff caught hold of her arm.

"No, don't change. We'll be there in no time."

He was right, but Rebecca vowed to be more careful. It made them seem like a little family, and they weren't. They went through the gate with the tickets Jeff had purchased.

"It's very expensive, isn't it?" Rebecca asked.

"All the rides are free if you're willing to stand in line. At least they don't nickel and dime you to death. All you have to pay for is food and Bill's in charge of that."

Joey was so excited he wanted to go in every direction. Jeff took charge and started them off to the left, where there was a pirate ship swinging in the air.

Both Chelsea and Rebecca opted out of that ride, but the men took Joey between them, promising his mother they'd bring him back safely.

"I think," Chelsea said after watching the ride, "if I'd gotten on that ride, I would've lost my breakfast."

"I made sure Joey ate his breakfast. I hope that wasn't a mistake."

"Now I'm doubly glad I didn't go on that ride."

"How about the sombrero ride? That's next. Will you go on it?"

"I think so. It doesn't look too bad."

Rebecca looked at the sombreros that spun around and around, like the teacup ride at Disneyland. "Do you think all five of us could fit in one sombrero?"

"I think so. It'd be a tight fit, but I don't object to squeezing in," Chelsea said with a smile. She wore jeans today and had tied her hair into a ponytail and looked about eighteen.

"You look good, today, Chelsea," Rebecca said.

"Thanks. So do you. But I'm glad you're not a blonde. You'd be too hard to compete with."

Rebecca wanted to assure Chelsea she wasn't competing with her, but the men came back from the boat ride without suffering any sickness.

Joey was ecstatic. "Mommy, it was great. I would've fallen out if Daddy hadn't held me in."

"What about me?" Bill demanded. "I held you in, too."

"Yeah. Uncle Bill held me in, too. And he wasn't even afraid I'd get sick, either. He said so."

"After the ride was over," Jeff added, and everyone laughed.

"Ready for the hat ride?" Jeff asked.

"I think we can all get in one sombrero," Chelsea said, looking at Bill from under her lashes.

"I'm all for a good squeeze," Bill agreed.

They got on the sombrero ride and it was a tight squeeze for them all to get in one, but they made it. Rebecca and Chelsea sat on each side of Joey and the men were closest to the gate. Rebecca noticed that Bill was with Chelsea and Jeff was with her. Their arms were around each other to make more room.

She was thrown against Jeff's chest several times, and he tightened his hold on her shoulder. They were almost in an embrace except for trying to protect Joey, whose face was aglow with excitement.

"He sure likes this amusement park, doesn't he?" Jeff whispered in her ear.

"Yes, but—I'm not sure this was a good idea. You should have Chelsea here next to you."

"I'm not complaining."

Rebecca didn't want to complain, either. She loved being in Jeff's arms, but her conscience told her she should complain and she should be uncomfortable with the way things kept ending up with this foursome. Before she could get up the nerve to talk to Jeff, the ride ended.

"I think I might have some broken knees after that ride," Bill complained. "I'm too tall to be scrunched up like that."

"The next ride won't scrunch you up," Jeff promised. "And it will cool you off."

"The log ride!" Chelsea shouted. "It's my favorite."

"What's a log ride?" Joey asked.

"We all get in a carved-out log and go on a water ride. You'll love it," Jeff told him.

They got in line and the closer they got to the ride, the more excited Joey got. "Can I be in front, Daddy? That's the best place."

"Only if I sit right behind you so I can hold on to you." Jeff looked at Rebecca. "Is that okay with you?"

"Of course."

"Good. You sit right behind me and hold on to me."

"Shouldn't Chelsea—"

"I'll hold on to Bill. He'll feel left out if no one holds on to him. Isn't that right, Bill?"

"You bet," Bill agreed, winking at Rebecca.

Rebecca smiled, but she wasn't sure she understood. Joey, Jeff and Rebecca all got in one log, then Chelsea and Bill got in the log ride behind them. Jeff drew Rebecca's arms around his waist. "Don't let loose, okay? If you do, I'll have to turn around and check on you and I might lose Joey."

She knew he was teasing, but she locked her arms around his middle and laid her head on his back. His hands patted hers right before the ride started.

"When's it going to get scary, Daddy? All we're doing is riding along smoothly."

"Just wait, son. There's a big finish."

Rebecca didn't look back at the other couple. She didn't want to see them holding on to each other. When they climbed the last hill before they zoomed down the log flume, splashing water everywhere, Joey began to get excited. "Are we almost there, Daddy?"

"We are, son. Get ready."

The quick ride down the flume left them all wet and laughing.

"I want to go again!" Joey screamed.

"Look at that line," Jeff said. "Maybe we'll do it again later. There are lots of other rides. I love the mine train."

"What's that, Daddy? Let's go ride it."

"Calm down, son. Let's get an ice cream and take the sky ride across the park."

They all got ice cream bars dipped in chocolate and rolled in nuts. Then they watched a fake western gun battle in the middle of the street. Joey sat on his father's shoulders so he could see clearly.

"You're probably going to have ice cream and chocolate in your hair, you know," Rebecca warned.

"I'll survive," he assured her, grinning.

She was fortunate that Jeff was such a tolerant parent. But then she'd always believed he would be a good daddy. Her plans, as a nineteen-year-old, had included several children after they'd married. But the twists of fate had changed that picture.

Her dreams couldn't come true for her, because Jeff was going to marry Chelsea. But her dreams would come true for Joey. He would have his daddy, just as she'd planned. But Chelsea would be the "mom" in the picture.

"Hey!" Jeff said, putting an arm around Rebecca's shoulder. "Did you see the gunfight?"

"Oh, yes, of course. Joey, you should get down from your dad's shoulders now. You didn't drip ice cream into his hair, did you?"

"I don't think so, Mommy," Joey said carelessly.

Rebecca gave an exasperated sigh. After he put Joey on the ground, Rebecca ordered Jeff to bend his head so she could check his hair herself. She picked out several pieces of chocolate and used her tissues to wipe up the ice cream.

"Okay, I think that's the best I can do."

Jeff thanked her. Then he kissed her on her lips.

"Jeff, don't do that!"

"Chelsea and Bill have walked on ahead and Joey's with them. Come on, we'll catch up." He grabbed her hand and started off after them.

Rebecca wrenched her hand free. "Jeff, you can't betray Chelsea like that."

Jeff came to a halt. "I'm not trying to hurt Chelsea."

"You don't have to try. I appreciate your acceptance of Joey and me, but Chelsea must be first. I know that."

"Just trust me, Becca. We'll work things out."

Again he took her hand and pulled her after him. They caught up with the other three in line for the ride that crossed over the park.

"Did you get all the ice cream out?" Chelsea asked with a smile.

"I tried. Joey wasn't very careful," Rebecca said, frowning at her son.

"I didn't mean to drip any, Mommy. Is it all right, Daddy?"

"Of course it is, Joey. Don't worry about it."

"You're letting him off too easy," Rebecca said with a warning in her voice.

"Get in, Mom, before we have to throw you overboard for ruining our fun," Jeff teased.

"No!" Joey called out in alarm. "We wouldn't hurt Mommy."

Jeff hugged his little boy. ''I was just teasing your mommy, Joey. I would never hurt her. I promise.''

Joey relaxed slightly, but he took his mother's hand and sat beside her. Rebecca's heart swelled with love at her son's protectiveness.

Jeff settled in beside them and put his arm on the backs of their seats. Chelsea and Bill settled on the other side. Again, Rebecca felt she should change places with Chelsea, but the car lifted off on the cable that stretched across the park.

Chapter Ten

As the car was coming in for a landing, Jeff pointed out his favorite ride to Joey. "See, over there, that's the mine train ride. Do you want to try it?"

"Yeah!" Joey said enthusiastically, trying to stand so he could see the ride better. Rebecca reminded her son to remain seated until they'd landed. Right now, Jeff was like the Pied Piper where Joey was concerned.

They all walked over to the entrance of the roller coaster ride. Joey had to measure himself against the sign and he just barely reached the height required. That was only because he was big for his age.

"Hurray—I can ride it, Mommy."

"Yes, you can, but I'm not going to ride it. Why don't you ride with Daddy and Chelsea?"

Jeff frowned. "These cars are kind of small. I'm not sure three of us will fit in. Besides, who would Bill ride with? I think it will work better if we split up in twos, if you're sure you don't want to ride?"

"I'm sure," Rebecca told him. "I'll sit on this bench and watch you ride. Keep hold of Joey."

"I will."

She backed away when it looked like Jeff intended to kiss her goodbye. A quick look showed her Chelsea had gone on ahead with Bill, but Rebecca wasn't taking any chances, even though her heart craved his kiss.

She sat down on the bench in the sunshine, enjoying a few minutes of rest alone. Then she caught sight of the train on which Joey and Jeff and Bill and Chelsea were going to ride. Bill settled in beside Chelsea and immediately put his arm around her, pulling her close. They were behind Jeff and Joey. Joey was busily telling his father something when the train took off, throwing him back against Jeff.

Rebecca caught glimpses of them then. She saw them as they climbed up high, going through an old mine cabin before they took the long plunge down into the water through a dark tunnel. Then the ride was over and everyone was getting out.

Some awkwardness between Bill and Chelsea caught Rebecca's eye, and she wondered what had happened. Chelsea's cheeks were flushed and she kept some distance between herself and Bill. Rebecca looked at Jeff to see if he noticed, but he was listening to his son rave about the ride.

When they reached Rebecca's side, Joey was begging to go on the ride again, but Bill and Chelsea were silent. Rebecca decided she needed to provide some assistance. "I'm really hungry. Don't you think we should take time for lunch?" She added a firm stare at Jeff.

"Oops, I guess you're right." When Joey complained, he added, "We don't want you getting sick again, young man, so we'd best mind your mommy."

They found a place that sold hamburgers. The women, along with Joey, picked out a picnic table and sat down to wait for Bill and Jeff to bring their food.

After a moment, Rebecca said, "Didn't you like that ride, Chelsea?"

Chelsea jumped several inches and looked away from Rebecca. "It was fun, but I'm glad you suggested lunch. I was getting tired."

"Yes. After this, I think the guys can try to win a stuffed toy for Joey while we watch. Then maybe I'll ride the merry-go-round with Joey. You three can go ride bumper cars. Then maybe Joey will be ready for some more rides without getting sick."

"That's a good plan. And I get my own bumper car."

"Well, of course." She saw the men coming and made another decision. "Joey, do you want to eat with Jeff and Chelsea?"

Joey immediately moved to Chelsea's side of the table, which of course meant Jeff would sit down there. Bill was left with no choice but to sit with Rebecca.

Jeff gave her a strange look as he sat down by Joey. He handed her her food while Bill handed Chelsea hers. Then Jeff set out Joey's hamburger and fries. "Hungry, Joey?"

"Yeah, I'm starved," the little boy said. "After we

eat, me and Mommy are going to ride the merry-go-round while you and Bill and Chelsea ride the bumper cars.''

''Is that so?'' Jeff asked, turning to stare at Rebecca. ''How does Mommy know I don't want to ride the merry-go-round, too?''

''Just a guess,'' Rebecca said with a smile, flashing a look at Chelsea. Then she stared at Jeff. ''I figured you and Chelsea might like to do something together.''

''I trust Bill to take Chelsea to the bumper cars if she wants. She understands that today is for Joey.''

''She's a little too understanding if you ask me,'' Rebecca said under her breath. She was trying to warn Jeff, but he seemed oblivious to what was going on.

After they'd eaten, they strolled over to the game area. Jeff tried to win Joey a huge stuffed bear. Instead, he only won a hand-sized bear.

''This size is better, Daddy,'' Joey assured his father. ''I wouldn't have room for such a big bear to sleep with me.''

Jeff picked up his son and gave him a big hug. At the stall two games down, Bill won a big doll in a satin dress. Chelsea had picked her out and it was obvious it was her prize. Rebecca nudged Jeff in the ribs, but he seemed to ignore the significance of their behavior.

''Let's go to the merry-go-round,'' Jeff said with enthusiasm.

''Okay!'' Joey agreed. ''I want to ride a big white horse.''

"Good, we'll find one for you." Taking Joey by the hand, Jeff headed down the midway, leaving the others to follow.

"I don't know which one's having more fun, Jeff or Joey," Bill said with a laugh.

"I know," Rebecca agreed. "Sorry, Chelsea, that he's so fixated on Joey."

"It's all right, Rebecca. Bill's taking good care of me. You're the one left out of things."

Once they reached the merry-go-round, Chelsea and Bill continued on to the bumper cars, leaving Rebecca to join Jeff and Joey just as the ride stopped and there was a wild scramble for the new riders to find their favorite mounts.

Joey found his white steed with flowers on his reins. The horse went up and down and had stopped at its highest spot. "Help me, Daddy. He's too tall."

"He'll come down, son. You have to hold on tight, okay?"

Next to his horse was one that didn't move. Jeff surprised Rebecca by taking her by the waist and placing her on its back.

"Jeff, I don't need to ride a horse."

"There's no reason for you to stand the entire ride. I'll stand between the two of you and keep you safe."

"I think you should be more concerned with keeping Chelsea safe," she warned.

"From what?"

"You mean from whom."

"I do?"

"Jeff, you can't be that blind. Can't you tell that

Bill has feelings for Chelsea?'' she demanded as the music started up and the horses began to move.

Joey called, "Daddy!" as his horse swooped down close to the floor and then rose up high again.

"I've got you, son. You're okay."

"But Chelsea—" Rebecca began again.

With one hand on Joey's back, Jeff put his other hand around Rebecca's waist and leaned forward and snatched a kiss. Then he whispered, "Chelsea is flirting with Bill, in case you hadn't noticed."

Rebecca stared at Jeff in surprise. He turned to Joey and teased him about his riding skills. What was Jeff doing? Did he want Chelsea to fall for Bill? And would she be wrong to read into that the hope that he wanted to marry her?

Rebecca shook her head no. She couldn't play a game that dangerous. Jeff had already broken her heart once. She couldn't give him another chance when she had no idea of his intentions.

Slipping down from her horse before Jeff could help her, she hurried out the gate ahead of him and Joey. Chelsea and Bill were waiting for them.

"Let's go up in the parachute ride next," Chelsea suggested.

Rebecca looked at her wide-eyed. "You *want* to go on that ride?"

"Oh, yes, it's lots of fun. And the view of the park is wonderful."

"Um, I think I'll just watch. I have a fear of heights."

"I want to ride it," Joey protested.

"Sorry, son," Jeff said. "I agree with your mommy on this one."

"We'll take him," Bill said at once. "It's not dangerous."

"Are you sure, Bill?" Rebecca asked. "I'm not sure how he'll react."

"We'll hold him in between us, Rebecca," Chelsea promised. "We'll bring him back safely."

After a quick look at Jeff's face, Rebecca nodded. "I suppose you can, just this once. But you do whatever they tell you to do, okay?"

"He will," Bill assured her. He took Joey's hand and Chelsea took his other hand and the three of them got in line for the ride.

"Come on, Becca, let's sit over here in the sunshine and watch them." He grabbed her hand to lead her in the direction he wanted to go.

She yanked her hand back. "Jeff, what are you doing? Chelsea might see you."

Jeff grinned at her. "Chelsea wasn't watching."

The fact that he had checked to determine if Chelsea was watching before he took her hand sent cold chills down Rebecca's spine. Was Jeff setting her up to be his mistress after he married Chelsea? It was a possibility, even though she found it hard to believe about Jeff.

But how well did she know him? She'd known him five years ago, but a lot had changed in five years. They sat down on the bench and he put his arm around her. She leaned forward so he couldn't actually touch her.

''Can you see them?'' she asked, straining to find the other couple and her son.

''Yes, they'll be put in the next parachute. That red one. Can you see them?''

''Yes, I see them now. Oh, I hope Joey doesn't get scared and freak them out. I should never have agreed to let him go.''

''It's too late now,'' Jeff said in cheerful tones.

She felt like smacking him. How could he be so careless about their son's safety? Maybe he was just pretending to care about her and Joey? Could that be it? She was feeling so confused about everything.

''Are we going to be invited to Joey's party?''

Rebecca turned to stare at him. ''What?''

''Are Bill, Chelsea and I going to be invited to Joey's birthday party? Or do we need to throw him our own party?''

''No. Please—there's only going to be one party. Of course you'll be invited if you want to come. But it might be right after preschool, like at one o'clock.''

''Chelsea is free then and Bill and I can clear our schedules for a couple of hours. That will be fine.''

''But Bill might not—''

He didn't let her finish. ''Yes, he does.''

''Does what?'' she snapped, tired of his high-handedness.

''Want to come.''

''How do you know?''

''Because he asked me what he should buy Joey for a present.''

''Oh.''

"Look. They're down. Joey's all safe and sound."

Rebecca couldn't believe she hadn't worried herself sick over Joey riding so high into the sky. The little boy saw them sitting on the bench and broke away from Bill and Chelsea, racing toward them.

He jumped into his mother's open arms, trying to tell her how amazing the ride was even as she checked him for broken bones.

Jeff stood and shook Bill's hand. "Good thing you brought him back safely, or I'd have to harm you."

Chelsea laughed. "Bill held on to him tightly. He said you'd kill him if he didn't."

Joey nodded. "Uncle Bill kept me safe, Mommy, I promise."

"I appreciate it, Bill," Rebecca said quietly, giving Joey one more hug.

"Well, now what?" Bill asked.

"The log ride! The log ride!" Joey said, jumping up and down.

"I did promise we'd do it a second time," Jeff reminded the others.

"*I* didn't promise," Rebecca said. "If you go again, I'll watch. I don't want to get wet again. It's cooling off. Being wet might not feel so good this time."

"I'll go again," Chelsea said. "It's one of my favorites. Rebecca, will you hold my doll for me? I don't want her to get wet."

"Of course I will. I can hold your bear, too, Joey, if you want."

"Okay."

They walked back across the park to the log ride. Rebecca found a bench in the sunshine and settled in with Joey's bear and Chelsea's doll. She didn't bother to point out to Jeff that he was again leaving his fiancée to his best friend's attentions. He apparently felt that was a good idea.

As the sun was setting, they headed to their car and drove back toward Dallas. Halfway back, Jeff stopped at a popular restaurant. "How about here for supper?"

"Surely you've spent enough on us today," Rebecca protested.

"Just what I like, a cheap date," Jeff said with a chuckle.

That remark caused Jeff and Bill to talk about the expensive ladies they'd dated. Neither Chelsea nor Rebecca seemed to be enjoying that conversational gambit, so they soon changed the topic.

After they started back toward home, Joey snuggled up against his mother and went to sleep. Since it was almost eight o'clock, his bedtime, she wasn't surprised. He was exhausted, of course, from their energetic day, but he had a smile on his face. She had no doubt that he'd enjoyed every minute of it.

For some reason, Jeff dropped Bill and Chelsea off at Bill's house. He'd promised to run Chelsea home so Jeff and Rebecca could get Joey to bed right away.

"Do you think that was wise?" she couldn't help asking in the darkened car as he drove to Vivian and Will's house.

"What?"

"Providing Bill with the opportunity to be alone with Chelsea?"

He grinned at her in the rearview mirror and said nothing. When they reached home, he parked the car and then came around to lift Joey out of the car and carry him inside. But he waited for Rebecca to get out of the car, too, before he started for the house.

Once they got Joey upstairs, Jeff helped undress him. Rebecca got a washcloth and cleaned Joey's face of the remnants of all he'd eaten that day.

"Think he'll be all right without a bath?"

"Yes, I think so. He can take one in the morning."

After Joey was tucked in, Rebecca walked Jeff back down the stairs. He stopped in the library for a moment to talk to Vivian and Will. Rebecca asked about Vanessa and learned that she'd had a date tonight with Jeremy, whom Will and Vivian had met for the first time.

"Did he seem nice?" Rebecca asked.

"I thought so," Vivian said, "but Will put the fear of God in him, so I'm not sure what he thought."

"Will?" Rebecca asked.

"He seemed nice enough. I just wanted him to know that Vanessa was owed a certain behavior."

Vivian and Rebecca laughed.

"Poor kid," Jeff said. "I know exactly how he felt. But if I ever have any girls, I'll do exactly the same thing."

"If you have daughters with Chelsea, they are certain to be beautiful."

"I don't think daughters with Rebecca would be

too ugly, either,'' Jeff said with a wry smile. Then, before anyone could comment on his remark, he bid them good-night. Rebecca walked him to the door, thanking him for Joey's day.

He leaned over and kissed her again. Then he shook his head and said, ''I'd better get out of here. Temptation is too great.''

Rebecca leaned her head against the door after she shut it. He was right. Temptation was great. How she longed for him to wrap his arms around her and give her one of those, deep soul-searching kisses they used to share. But it wouldn't be right. He was engaged to Chelsea, and she had no intention of playing the role of mistress, not even for Jeff.

With a quiet sigh, she went upstairs to bed.

JUST AS BETTY HAD SAID, Joey's birthday party was organized and invitations went out on Monday to his classmates, despite the short amount of time for the parents to respond. Joey was so excited about the idea he could scarcely stand it. It was his only topic of conversation. He asked questions about every detail and he speculated on what he would receive for gifts.

Rebecca, afraid he was thinking too much about himself, had him help her pick out prize gifts for the winners of the games. He enjoyed that immensely until his mother told him he couldn't win any prizes. As host, that would be rude. It took a while to get that idea across.

When she finally pointed out that all his friends would be bringing presents for him, he agreed to share. They even picked out small toys to go in a favor bag for each child to take home with him. Vivian had assured her that was standard these days. Vivian had offered to foot the bill for the party, but Rebecca told her she had some money saved from her job.

Wednesday evening, they put together the party favors and left them lined up on Betty's cabinet. Betty had mixed up the chicken salad for the sandwiches on Wednesday. She promised she would make the sandwiches, with the crusts cut off, of course, the next morning. The hot dogs had all been purchased, along with the buns and roasting sticks—actually long forks. They were going to build a fire in the barbecue pit, and Peter promised to supervise the area so he could keep a sharp eye out for any problems. When Joey learned they could roast marshmallows, too, he was thrilled.

"Can we make s'mores?" he asked eagerly.

"Not this time. You're having ice cream and cake. That will be enough sugar for a day or two."

"But, Mommy, we don't have a cake," Joey said, frowning, worried the highlight of his party would go missing.

"Betty is going to make you a special cake. Be sure to thank her for it."

"I will. But what if it's not—you know, decorated?" Joey asked.

"I think you can trust Betty. She knows all about birthday parties."

Rebecca was glad to send Joey off to school the

next morning. His teacher could deal with those endless questions. Rebecca took the day off from her own classes and work so she could ease Betty's burden somewhat. When she found Vivian setting the big dining table for the party, she suggested they move it to the patio.

"I'm so afraid they'll spill something on the carpet."

"Not to worry. We're not serving Kool-Aid. I learned that when I gave Vanessa her first party. We had to recarpet the entire dining room."

"Oh, no."

"Now we serve ginger ale. Those spills clean up easily."

"But we have eighteen children coming and there are only twelve chairs."

"Peter is bringing in a folding table with six more chairs. And we'll serve the mothers in the lounge, away from the noise of the party. They'll enjoy it more in there."

Rebecca gave Vivian a quick hug. "You and Betty are the best."

"You and Vanessa will run the party with Betty's help and I'll entertain the mothers. Will will float between the two groups, and Peter's in charge of the barbecue pit. I'm sure Chelsea will probably be a big help, too, along with Jeff and Bill, so I think we have everything covered."

"Yes. I'll go help Betty make the chicken salad sandwiches. When I was in there last, she was decorating a beautiful cake for Joey."

"Yes, she's good at cake making."

When it was almost time for the kids to arrive from school, the doorbell rang. Rebecca ran to answer it. Instead of the kids, it was Chelsea, Jeff and Bill. She made them welcome and asked for their assistance. Bill and Jeff she assigned to Peter during the roast. Chelsea agreed to join her and Vanessa in patrolling the dining room. All the presents would be in the lounge where they would join the other adults for the final event of the party. They would play games on the patio.

Three hours later, when all their short guests had departed with their mothers, everyone else collapsed in the lounge. Joey was still raring to go and admiring his presents. Rebecca served the adults leftover sandwiches, hot dogs, cake and ice cream as a reward for a job well done.

"I can't thank everyone enough for what you did today. This was Joey's first birthday party and it was so much fun for him."

Jeff added, "I thank you, too. And if I ever decide to give my son a party, remind me of this one. I'm sure I'll cancel it at once."

Joey leaped to his feet and ran to his father's side. "Didn't you have fun, Daddy?"

Jeff looked into those blue eyes so like his mother's and said, "Of course I had fun, but I'm very tired now. Aren't you?"

"No. I had two pieces of cake."

"At least," Rebecca murmured.

"Everyone's invited to dinner this evening," Vivian announced. "But I'm going upstairs to have a nap until then."

"Dinner?" Bill asked. "I don't feel like I can ever eat again. I had an eating contest with that big boy. What was his name?"

"I think it was Stephen," Chelsea said. "I couldn't believe you could be so childish."

"Hell, I thought I'd beat him easy. That kid ate four hot dogs."

Joey looked up, bright-eyed. "Hell, he always does."

There was a shocked silence. Then Rebecca took Joey's hand and led him from the room to discuss the issue of cursing.

Chapter Eleven

Bill, his cheeks red, apologized at once.

Will laughed. "Thanks for reminding me that I'll need to curb my language at all times. It's so easy to forget."

"I'm sure his mother will be reading Joey the riot act," Jeff added. "There's no harm done. Now, who wants to have a cake-eating contest? I'm feeling like I could manage another piece. Betty makes a damn fine cake."

Since Jeff had intentionally used a swearword to make Bill feel better, he was relieved when everyone laughed. Of course, he'd taken care to do so while his son and Rebecca were out of the room.

When Rebecca and Joey came back into the room, Rebecca announced, "Joey is going upstairs to his room for a nap. But he wanted to say something first."

"Thank you all for coming to my party and helping Mommy and everything. I appreciate it." Then he ran around the room, hugging everyone's neck.

"You'd better stop off in the kitchen and thank Betty and Peter, too," Jeff suggested.

"I will, Daddy. And you'll be here for supper, won't you?" Joey asked anxiously.

"Of course I will."

Fortunately, in Rebecca's mind, Jeff didn't mention that he, Bill and Chelsea had yet to give Joey a present. They thought it would be better to wait until after the party.

She'd agreed, but she didn't need Joey to get all excited again before she tried to get him to rest.

When she came back downstairs again, she discovered the other adults had put their heads together to decide how to spend the afternoon. Will and Vivian had recently gone to the movies and seen a movie they thought was good. Will suggested the four of them go to the movies while Joey rested.

"But I might not get back before he wakes up," Rebecca protested.

"True, but I'll be here, as will Betty and Peter, and he does have a lot of new toys to play with."

"Come on, Rebecca," Jeff urged. "I've been wanting to see that movie."

"Why don't the three of you go? I'll stay here and help clean up."

Will stood. "I insist you go, Rebecca. You worked hard all day for the party. You deserve a break."

Then he shooed them out the door.

When they got to the movie, the guys bought them popcorn and sodas. When they filed into the dark room, Rebecca discovered she was in the lead. Jeff

put a hand on her waist to guide her. When they found
seats, Jeff and Chelsea sat in the middle, with Rebecca and Bill on the outsides. Rebecca wished she
was on Chelsea's side, not Jeff's—it was too dangerous.

The movie started almost at once. It had been five
years since she'd been to a movie with Jeff. When
his hand reached over to take hers, she was so
wrapped up in the movie, she almost didn't think to
protest. When she realized what he'd done, she jerked
her hand away.

He gave an audible sigh but said nothing. She
didn't dare steal a look at Chelsea. Instead, she stared
straight ahead and sat stiffly in her seat. The movie
was ruined for her.

When they got back in the car, the two men talked
about the movie, but she noticed Chelsea didn't have
much to say about it. Rebecca said nothing, either. At
the house, the other three took in their presents for
Joey. The little boy met them at the door.

"I was afraid you'd forget to come back," he told
his daddy.

"Not a chance, squirt. I said I'd be here for dinner,
didn't I?"

"But it's almost ready."

"Then you'd better open these presents in a
hurry," Jeff told his son, watching him squeal with
delight and run into the library to tell Vivian and Will
that he had more presents.

When Will and Vivian handed him a gift also, and

Betty and Peter came in with their gift, Joey was completely overwhelmed.

"Where's Vanessa?" Rebecca asked.

"I'm here," Vanessa answered, coming in the door. "You don't think I'd miss Joey's second party, do you?"

She, too, handed Joey a package. Joey immediately hugged her neck. The others complained that they hadn't received a hug. Joey again made the rounds, hugging everyone. He was so excited he didn't even know what he was doing.

Rebecca had him come sit beside her and she gave him one present at a time to open, telling him who it was from so he could properly thank them. She knew her son wouldn't appreciate her gift much, since it was clothes. But she'd tried to buy him the things his friends wore to school. When he opened Jeff's present, he was speechless. His father had purchased a watch for him to wear.

"I figured it was time for you to learn to tell time," he said.

"Thank you, Daddy. Will you teach me?"

"Look, it says six-thirty."

When all the presents had been opened, Betty called them all to dinner. They settled around the dining table for a leisurely meal. Rebecca kept an eye on Joey, who sat beside her, as usual. His eyelids began to sag partway through dinner. She urged him to stay awake so they could sing happy birthday to him when Betty brought in another birthday cake she'd made. This one was chocolate with white icing, Joey's favorite.

Joey ate the small piece he received. Then he leaned against his mother, yawning.

"Are you ready for bed, sweetie?"

"Yes, Mommy. This has been the best birthday ever."

"I agree. Why don't you tell everyone thank you and good-night, and I'll take you up to bed?"

He did as he was told, and Rebecca picked him up. Jeff stood and took him from his mother. "I'll carry him upstairs for you."

Rebecca had hoped to avoid being alone with Jeff. Now, once Joey went to sleep, she would have to hurry back downstairs or be faced with time alone. She did so, almost tripping in her rush. Jeff caught her arm, saving her from a fall.

"What's your hurry, Becca?"

"I want to help Betty clean up. It's been a long day for all of us."

"I don't think you have to hurry that much. I bet everyone will still be sitting around the table. You didn't eat any of the cake yet."

"I thought I should skip it. Too many calories."

"Joey would want you to eat a piece."

She ignored him and rushed into the dining room.

"Come sit down, Rebecca," Vivian said at once. "We've cut you a piece of cake. Did Joey go right to sleep?"

"Yes, he was asleep before I could wash his face.

Thank you all for giving him such a wonderful day. I think he'll remember it for all his life.''

``It was fun for us, too,'' Will assured her. ``Joey has brought a lot of joy to this house.''

After a few minutes, when she'd finally finished her piece of cake, Bill, Chelsea and Jeff excused themselves. Rebecca got up and gave Chelsea a hug.

``Thanks for helping us today, Chelsea. You were really good with the kids.''

``I surprised myself,'' Chelsea said with a laugh. ``I didn't know I could relate to four-year-olds.''

``You certainly can. You all were terrific, especially Bill with the roasting marshmallows. I saw him comforting more than one child who lost his marshmallow in the fire.''

Bill blushed and grinned at the same time. ``You'd have thought the world had ended. All it took was a new marshmallow.''

``It's nice when tragedies can be so easily solved,'' Rebecca agreed, avoiding looking at Jeff.

Once they'd left, she went back in to help Betty with the dinner dishes. Vanessa, too, was helping out. They dried the dishes together. After a few minutes, Vanessa said, ``Are you feeling all right?''

``Yes, just tired.''

``I guess so. You've had a long day.''

``Everyone has.'' She put away a plate. ``Joey was so happy. I can't thank you enough for all you did.''

``We love him almost as much as you do, sis.''

``That's what is even more impressive. For almost

his entire life, there was just the two of us. And now his life is filled with so many people.''

"Chelsea is nicer than I thought she'd turn out to be,'' Vanessa said.

"Yes, she is. I—I hope she and Jeff will be happy together.''

"You still love him, don't you?'' Vanessa asked softly.

Rebecca's head jerked up. She met Vanessa's gaze and then looked away. "It doesn't matter. He's going to marry Chelsea.''

"I'm sorry, sis. It would've been better if it had turned out differently.''

"Yes, but it didn't. I'll survive.''

"I know you will. I'm never going to marry. We'll get a big condo and share it.''

"Why would you never marry? I thought you were half in love with Jeremy.''

"Dear Jeremy thought since it was our first date, I should thank him by going to bed with him.''

"No! Even after Will gave him a talking-to?''

"Even after he'd been flirting with me like he was shy.''

"How terrible of him. I'm glad you ditched him. You did ditch him, didn't you?''

"Oh, yes. If I can't find someone with more sensitivity than Jeremy, I'll never marry.''

"Hopefully, some really great guy will come along and change your mind. I'd really like to have some nieces and nephews.''

Vanessa put her cup towel away and hugged Rebecca again. "Don't hold your breath. Maybe Will will find Rachel or David, and they'll produce some children."

"Or maybe Jim."

"I don't know. He's thirty-one and not married. Sounds like he may be going solo, too."

"Maybe he just hasn't had time to settle down. He wrote in his last letter that he's thinking about getting out of the marines when it's time for him to re-up, which will be in six months. I'd hoped he'd come home sooner than that."

"Me, too. But at least he writes nice letters."

"Yes, he does." Rebecca hung up her cup towel also. "I think I'm going to go up to bed now. I'm tired."

"Me, too," Vanessa said.

They both stopped off in the library to tell Will and Vivian good-night. Then they climbed the stairs together.

AT THE OFFICE THE NEXT afternoon, Rebecca hurried in to work, sure she'd have a lot of filing piled up since she hadn't worked yesterday.

"Hi, Harriet. Thank you for sending a present for Joey. That was so sweet of you. He loves that toy."

"I'm so glad. I've nephews who are a couple of years older than your Joey and I asked for their opinion."

"Well, tell them they did a great job. I'll get started right away with the filing," she said, hurrying past Harriet's desk to her own.

"Jeff wants to see you first."

"Why?" Rebecca demanded sharply.

Harriet gave her a reproving look. "I didn't ask him, dear."

"Oh, no, of course not. I'm sorry, Harriet. You took me by surprise. Are you sure he's free now?"

"Oh, yes, he's waiting."

Left with no choice, Rebecca advanced toward Jeff's closed door like a heroine in the tumbrel approaching the guillotine. She knocked on the door and prayed he wouldn't answer. But, of course, he did. "Come in."

She opened the door but didn't go in. "You wanted to see me about something?"

"Yes, come on in and have a seat."

"Why?"

After giving her a considering look, Jeff got up from his desk and came to the door. He took her by the arm and pulled her into his office and closed the door.

"I'd appreciate it if you didn't act like I had the plague."

"I wasn't—"

"Yes, you were. I wanted to remind you that the basketball tickets are for Saturday night. Do you want to go to dinner first?"

"No. No, it will be better if Joey has his dinner at home, before he gets too excited."

"That actually makes sense. But I'll need to pick you up by seven. Can you be ready by then?"

"Yes. Aren't you picking up Chelsea and Bill, too?"

"No." He cleared his throat. "Bill wanted to go to a steak place and Chelsea thought that was a good idea."

"You'll go with them, won't you?" She watched him with worried eyes.

"I don't think so. I get tired of eating out."

"Jeff, you have to go with them."

"No, I don't. In fact, since you refuse to go, I'm going to see if I can talk Vivian into inviting me for dinner."

"That's not fair or polite. You know she'll invite you to dinner at the first hint."

"I know. That's one of the things I love about her."

"Jeff, I don't think you're thinking clearly. You need to go with Chelsea."

"Honey, you're the one who isn't thinking clearly. Maybe you'd better get back to work before I say more than I should."

Finding herself easily dismissed, on the other side of the closed door, Rebecca thought of several things she could say, but she didn't go back in. Instead, she got to work and said a few prayers as she did so.

CHELSEA PICKED AT HER STEAK, not really eating it.

"Aren't you hungry?" Bill asked.

"No, I'm not. I don't think this was a good idea."

"Going to the basketball game? I think it will be fun."

"No. Having dinner without Jeff and Rebecca. It's too—too intimate."

Bill straightened and stared at Chelsea. "You're afraid I'll do something out of line? Jeff is my friend, and as long as that ring is on your finger, you're safe. I make no promises if you should give back the ring. Then I would feel free to express my emotions about you. But not until then."

"Bill, that's not how it works."

"It is for me."

"I don't mean about you being honorable. My parents—"

"What about your parents?"

"They expect a wedding. We've been planning it for six months already."

"Did you think I'd offer you an affair?"

"Bill, you don't understand. You're not—you graduated from Texas A&M. That's not a socially elite school. Jeff graduated from SMU. His uncle was well-known and had an upstanding reputation."

Bill froze. Then he said, "Are you telling me I'm not good enough for you and your parents?"

"Not me! It doesn't matter to me. But my parents—they make things difficult." She bowed her head, unwilling to meet his fiery gaze.

"Well, you don't have to worry, do you, Chelsea. You're all set, engaged to the socially acceptable Jeff Jacobs. I wish you happiness, sweetheart. That ought to be quite a marriage of socially acceptable people." Then he waved to the waiter. "Check, please."

"But—sir, is there something wrong with your steaks?" the waiter asked, confused.

"No, they're just fine."

"Do you want a to-go box?"

"No, thank you. We're running late."

"I'll bring your check immediately." The waiter hurried away.

"Why are you doing this?" Chelsea demanded.

"I don't want to risk diminishing your reputation by being seen with me." His jaw was squared, his teeth clenched.

"Bill," Chelsea pleaded, tears in her eyes. "It's my parents who believe that, not me. It's just that to change things now will cause a big row."

"We have no more need to discuss our situation, Chelsea, because it doesn't exist. I thought you were courageous, but I was wrong. Forget I ever told you I care about you."

"Here's your check, sir," the waiter said as he hurried breathlessly to the table.

Bill looked at the check, opened his wallet and pulled out a couple of bills, including a generous tip. Then, saying thank you, he stood and waved Chelsea in front of him, but he didn't touch her.

In the darkness of the car, Chelsea tried to talk to Bill, but he would say nothing. They got to the arena early. When they claimed their seats, Bill sat there in silence, staring at everything in the arena but Chelsea.

OF COURSE, JEFF WAS INVITED to dinner, as Rebecca had predicted. They ate at six so he, Rebecca and Joey could leave for the basketball game on time.

Joey was still rather confused. "How come I can't play ball with them?" he asked his father again.

"You'll understand when you see these men play. To start with, they're very big."

"Bigger than you?"

"I'm afraid so. And very skilled with the basketball. It's time to go. Where's your mother?"

"I'm right here," Rebecca said from behind him.

He turned and stood there staring at her. "Wow. Everyone's going to be watching you, not the game. You look terrific."

"Thank you. I thought this would be appropriate," she said, waving to her outfit. She'd put on a three-quarter-length wool skirt, a red blouse and a black vest.

"Oh, it's very appropriate. Come on. We don't want to be late."

There was a huge crowd at opening night, but, of course, their seats were reserved. Bill and Chelsea were already there. Jeff sat down beside Chelsea; Joey took the seat next to him; and Rebecca sat in the third seat. They were in the first row, almost on the basketball court. Immediately after they sat down, there was a huge roar as the home team came out for their shoot-around.

Joey stared at the tall men with his mouth open. Then he turned to Rebecca. "Look, Mommy, they're giants."

"Yes, they are, sweetie. Remember Daddy said they could handle the ball really well? Watch them."

After a couple of minutes, Joey turned to his father, asking him to explain the game. That explanation took several minutes, leaving Rebecca free to take in the electric atmosphere.

She glanced over at Chelsea and Bill. They didn't seem to be happy with each other. A minute later, Chelsea leaned over and told Rebecca she was going to the rest room. She asked if Rebecca wanted to accompany her.

"Yes, I will." She leaned toward Jeff to tell him where she was going so Joey wouldn't get upset. He had his arm on the back of their seats and leaned toward her. Just then a camera flashed in their eyes.

Chapter Twelve

"What was that?" Rebecca demanded.

"Just ignore it. They take random pictures of the audience."

Rebecca stood and joined Chelsea. When they reached the rest room, they found it almost empty. When Rebecca came out of her stall, Chelsea was powdering her nose in front of the mirror.

"You look very nice tonight," Rebecca said.

"I like your outfit, too," Chelsea said with a slight smile.

"We're just an admiration society, aren't we?" Rebecca said with a laugh.

"Rebecca," Chelsea said, her voice serious, "did you ever do something your parents didn't like? I mean something important?"

Rebecca looked at Chelsea and realized her reason for asking was important. "Yes, I did. When I discovered I was pregnant with Joey, my parents were very upset. They wanted me to get an abortion, and when I said I wouldn't, they refused to have anything to do with me ever again. So I left them to set up my life alone with Joey.''

''Oh. That's really serious.''

''Yes, it was, but I don't regret my decision.'' After a moment of silence, Rebecca asked, ''Does that help?''

''Yes. I just have to find some courage.''

''Chelsea, do you remember saying you didn't realize you could relate to four-year-olds? Well, I think you have a lot of courage in you, too. You just haven't looked for it yet.''

''Do you think so?''

''Yes, I do. I didn't want to like you, you know. But I do. I think you're a terrific person, and I wouldn't think that if you were a coward.''

Chelsea hugged her. ''Thank you, Rebecca. You're a wonderful person and the best friend I've ever had.''

She wiped her eyes with a tissue and the two ladies returned to the basketball game.

As soon as Rebecca left his side, Jeff was approached by the man with the camera.

''Mr. Jacobs, mind telling me your companion's name? The picture will probably be in the *Park Cities News*.''

''No, I'd rather not. And I think it would be better if the picture didn't appear in the paper.''

''A secret, Mr. Jacobs?''

''Go away and leave us alone,'' Jeff ordered.

Bill, who had been ignoring everyone to his right, turned and looked at his friend. "Is there a problem?"

"That jerk took a picture for the local paper and wanted Rebecca and Joey's names. I refused to give them to him. Chelsea's parents may get upset if they see that picture."

"Can't you just explain you were taking your son to a basketball game?"

"You've never met them."

"No, I haven't. What's wrong with them?"

"They're rigid, difficult, and they also happen to be snobs."

Bill stared straight ahead. "I figured that out tonight. Did you know they don't think much of a Texas A&M graduate?"

Jeff laughed. "They obviously don't know anything about your family, if you're referring to yourself."

"I am. I figured they wouldn't know. You know I don't go around bragging about my family's finances or the fact that my father is a senator."

"Why are we talking about this? Did Chelsea—I didn't think she—"

"I gather she's afraid of disappointing her parents."

"That would be hard for Chelsea."

"Not if she has any courage," Bill said, his jaw firming.

"Chelsea's just learning to live outside their restrictions. She doesn't start with giant steps," Jeff said softly.

"Daddy, look. There's more giants." Joey was pointing to the other end of the court.

"Yes, son, that's the other team."

Just then, Chelsea and Rebecca returned to their seats. Jeff looked at the serious expression on Rebecca's face. "Is everything okay?"

"Yes, fine. When does the game start?"

He gave her another long look, but he said nothing else.

When the game ended, after a rousing win by the home team, Jeff turned to Chelsea and Bill to say good-night.

"Jeff, may I beg a ride home?" Chelsea asked.

Jeff stared at Chelsea and then Bill. Neither of them gave a clue about what was wrong, but Jeff noted Bill didn't make a protest.

"Of course you can," Rebecca said, preempting Jeff's answer.

"Sure," Jeff added, but he was watching his friend.

Bill simply said, "I'll see you Monday, Jeff. Good game tonight." Then he turned and walked away.

Jeff wanted to ask Chelsea what went wrong, but he couldn't do that in front of Rebecca. "Do you mind if I take Rebecca and Joey home first? It's past his bedtime."

"It won't take much longer to drop Chelsea off. Joey can manage," Rebecca said from the back seat.

Chelsea said, "I'd prefer to be dropped off first, if it's okay."

Once he'd dropped Chelsea off, walking her to the

door, he got back in the car, noting that Joey was asleep. "What happened?" he asked.

"I'm not sure. She asked me if I'd ever done something my parents didn't approve of. Something important."

"And your answer?"

After a moment in the darkness of the car, she gave her answer. "My parents wanted me to get an abortion. They were willing to forgive and forget if I did so. I refused, so they kicked me out."

Jeff parked the car in front of Will and Vivian's house and sat there in the darkness. "You have a lot of courage, Rebecca."

"No, I had a lot of love, for you and for the child we'd created. I couldn't do what they asked and continue to live."

"And do you still have any of that love left?"

"I love Joey with every ounce of my being."

"You know that's not what I'm asking."

"And you know that you have no right to ask that question when you've promised to marry someone else." She opened the door, got out of the car and pulled Joey up into her arms.

"I'll carry him," Jeff said, getting out of the car.

"No. Tonight I'll take him to bed. You can go." She turned her back on him and left him standing there.

SUNDAY MORNING, Rebecca found out who had taken the picture at the game. The small local paper put out a Sunday edition with a section about who had been seen where. There, at the bottom of the first page, was the picture of her and Jeff, leaning toward each other, with Joey between them.

Underneath the picture the paper wrote, ''Local lawyer Jeff Jacobs seen at the opening of the pro basketball season with an unknown beauty and a little boy.''

''Oh, my,'' Vivian said when she first saw the picture. ''This is a nice picture of the three of you, but it completely cuts out Chelsea.''

''Yes, it does. I hope it doesn't cause trouble for her,'' Rebecca said solemnly.

''It could. Her parents are rather difficult.''

''I gathered that from something Chelsea said. She's such a nice person. She deserves better parents.''

''So did you,'' Will said.

''Yes, but they weren't my real parents. Chelsea's not adopted, is she?''

Will laughed. ''No, she's not. But she is a nice person. I thought she might be like them, but she's not.''

''No. Joey likes her very much.'' Rebecca smiled at her son, sitting beside her eating his breakfast.

''Well, we'll hope it won't cause any difficulty. I'm sure Jeff can explain that Chelsea was on his other side.''

''Yes.'' But Rebecca was thinking about the trip to the rest room with Chelsea, and the unhappiness between her and Bill. What had she been asking? Did it have something to do with Bill?

Jeff called a short time later. He'd seen the picture and wanted to know if she'd seen it.

"Yes, Vivian showed me."

"You're not upset about it, are you?"

"No, but I'm worried about Chelsea."

"I'm going to call her now."

"If there's anything I can do to help her, please let me know."

"Rebecca—yes, I will." Jeff hung up the phone.

Rebecca didn't hear from him again. She guessed either Chelsea wasn't upset, or there wasn't anything she could do.

JEFF CAME TO WORK MONDAY morning, feeling uneasy. He'd talked briefly to Chelsea, but she said nothing to him and refused any offer to speak to her parents.

Bill was already in his office and Jeff stopped by the door. "Bill, have you talked to Chelsea?"

"No."

"Did you see the picture of me, Joey and Rebecca in the paper?"

"Yeah, I saw it. Did you think it would upset her parents?"

"I'm pretty sure it would, but she wouldn't talk to me about it when I called yesterday."

"I can't tell you anything."

"You could tell me what happened Saturday night when you went to dinner." Jeff stood there, staring at his friend.

"Chelsea and I were talking about my schooling

and she made the comment that I wouldn't be an acceptable person in the husband category because I graduated from A&M and that's not as classy as SMU.''

''I'd hate for your father to hear that opinion.''

A bark of laughter broke from Bill. ''Yeah, me, too.''

Just then, Harriet entered the office. ''Morning, Harriet.''

''Good morning. Nice picture of you and Rebecca and little Joey in the paper.''

''Thanks,'' Jeff said with a wry grin, and went into his office.

An hour later, Jeff was immersed in paperwork when he heard Harriet say, ''Why, good morning, Rebecca. What are you doing here so early?''

Jeff immediately headed for the outer office, where he could see Rebecca standing there, dressed more formally than she usually dressed. He wondered what was up.

''Rebecca, what's wrong?'' Jeff asked, even as he noted Bill coming to the door of his office, too.

''Well, first of all, I'm not Rebecca,'' the woman said, and Jeff knew at once it wasn't a lie. There was a slight difference in her voice.

''I beg your pardon, ma'am. You look a lot like her.''

''I assume she's the person in this picture?'' the woman asked, showing the photo in the folded newspaper.

''Yes, that's Rebecca. May I ask your name?''

"Rachel Morgan."

"Rachel," Jeff said, excitement building in him. "I'm sorry. You look remarkably like someone else we know. Were you adopted, by any chance?"

The question bothered her. "How dare you ask such a personal question? Why do you ask?"

"Because Rebecca, the woman in the picture who looks just like you, was adopted. She recently discovered she had a twin who was split up from her and went to another family."

"Her twin?" Rachel said sharply.

"Yes. Harriet, call Will and ask him to get over here as soon as he can."

Rachel looked at Harriet and then back at Jeff. "Who is Will?"

"He's the stepfather of Vanessa, your youngest sister, if you're who I think you are. She was adopted when she was only three months old. Her mother wanted her to have more family, so she hired Will to find Vanessa's siblings. So far he's only found Rebecca and Jim, but—"

"How is he her stepfather?"

"He married Vanessa's mother."

"How—tidy. How—how many siblings were there?"

"Three girls and three boys. One of the brothers is dead. He was serving in the military and was killed serving his country. His name was Walter, but they called him Wally."

There was a flash of something in the woman's eyes that made Jeff wonder if she had a distant memory. He continued to bring her up to date. "The oldest boy, Jim, is still in the military, too, on assignment in the Middle East, but he and your—I mean the other girls have been corresponding with him—they think he'll be home in six months."

"The other boy?"

"They haven't found him yet. His name is—was David."

"Can I—I meet this Rebecca?"

"Yes, she works here in the afternoons. But I think Will will want to invite you back to his and Vivian's house. If he does that, I'll go get Rebecca. She's in class right now. And they can call Vanessa."

"May I sit down?" she suddenly asked.

"Right here, dear," Harriet said. She gestured to a chair against the wall.

"I've often suspected that I was adopted and confronted my mother about it a couple times, but she'd always denied it. She told me I wasn't—that I was always her child."

"Why did you ask that question?" Will asked as he heard her words upon his entry.

"Rachel, this is Will Greenfield, the P.I. Vivian hired and later married." Jeff shook Will's hand.

"I asked that question because she didn't have any pictures of me until my third birthday. She said she couldn't afford film when I was a baby."

"And what did your father say?" Will asked, sitting down beside her.

"By that time they had divorced. He never called

or came back after he left. He never paid any child support, either.''

She sounded bitter, and Jeff and Will exchanged looks. Then Will leaned toward her. ''I'd like to take you to meet my wife. We'll get Vanessa and Rebecca home as quick as we can, and Jeff can join us for lunch.''

''I don't want to cause any inconvenience.''

''Rachel, we went all the way to Arkansas to find Rebecca. Adding an extra plate at lunch isn't an inconvenience.''

''She was in Arkansas? How did she get there?''

''That's where her adoptive parents lived.''

''And she just left them and came down here?''

Jeff stepped in. ''She and her parents had already parted ways. She was pregnant and they kicked her out of their home.''

''Did she have the baby?''

''Yes. She had a son. My son. Boy, this is getting complicated, huh? Joey is four now.''

Will took over the conversation again. ''Come with me, Rachel, and we'll get the girls home for lunch. We can compare notes and break it all down for you. It's a lot of information to take in all at once. But once you see Rebecca, I don't think you'll have any doubts that you two are twins.''

''That's why I'm here,'' she said, pointing to the picture. ''I wanted to find out who she was. She looks so much like me.''

''Yes, she does.''

"All right, I'll come to lunch. I have my car. Shall I follow you?"

"That will be fine. Jeff, can you go to the school and try to track down Rebecca? Vivian will call Vanessa." Will led Rachel out of the office.

Bill stepped forward. "I couldn't believe that wasn't Rebecca."

"There's a difference in their voices. But that was about the only difference. It's remarkable." Then he turned to Harriet. "Do you have Rebecca's class schedule?"

"Yes, I do." She dug through some papers and pulled out Rebecca's schedule.

Jeff noted her class location and immediately told Harriet he would be back after lunch. Then he headed for the university, only a few blocks away, to find Rebecca.

When he reached the classroom, Rebecca had twenty minutes left of the class. He could wait until it was over, but he was impatient and imagined Rebecca would be, too, if she knew the situation.

He stepped into the classroom and immediately spotted Rebecca. Then he approached the professor. "I apologize for interrupting your class, but Rebecca Barlow has a family emergency. I hope you'll excuse her."

"And you are?"

"Jeff Jacobs, her family's attorney."

"Very well. Ms. Barlow, you are excused."

Rebecca had already packed up her books. Her cheeks were pale, and she hurried down to Jeff, questions in her eyes. He took her elbow and guided her quickly out of the class. "Joey is fine, everyone is fine. Don't look so panicked."

"Then what's the emergency?"

"We think we've found Rachel."

"Rachel? What? My twin? What are you talking about? How did you find her?"

"That's the amazing thing. She saw that picture in the paper and wanted to know who you were because you both look so similar. She doesn't know if she's adopted or not. She'd asked her mother, but her mother had told her she wasn't. Will has taken her home and they're trying to reach Vanessa."

"Did you bring your car?"

"Yes."

"Well, let's go."

RACHEL MORGAN SAT ON THE SOFA, talking to Vivian and Will. She felt like she'd fallen down a rabbit hole like Alice in Wonderland. Her life had been turned upside down a month ago, and now it was taking on yet another turn. She was discovering the possibility that she'd been adopted and had a twin sister...and four other siblings.

"I'm sorry. I'm a little overwhelmed," she finally said.

"I'm sure you are, dear. But when you meet Rebecca and Vanessa, you'll see why we're so sure you are their sister."

Rachel managed a smile. Then they all heard the front door close.

"Mom? I got your message and rushed right home. Where are you?"

"It's Vanessa," Vivian said. Will put a hand on her shoulder to keep her from standing. He went to the door. "In here, Vanessa."

"Will, Mom said—"

"Yes. She's in here."

Vanessa pushed past Will into the room. Then she stopped and stared. "Oh, my!"

"Hello," Rachel said slowly, assessing the young woman's appearance. She looked a great deal like Rachel, but not identical. This was the one that was three years younger. This young woman had been raised in this spectacular house, well fed, well dressed, and well educated.

"Hello. I'm Vanessa."

"Yes, I know."

"Your name is Rachel?"

"Yes. Rachel Morgan."

Vanessa reluctantly took her eyes off Rachel. "Where's Rebecca? Isn't she here yet?"

"No. Jeff went to get her. Is that a car I hear outside?" Vivian asked, leaning forward.

Vanessa ran to the window. "Yes, it's Jeff and Rebecca." She turned and left the room. In a moment Vanessa returned with the two of them.

Rebecca froze as soon as she entered the room. So did Rachel. The two young women stared at each other, astounded by the similarities in their looks. Eventually Rebecca walked closer and closer until they were face-to-face. "It's like looking in a mirror," Rebecca said softly.

"I think you look younger than me," Rachel said.

"No, I think we look the same."

"Do *you* believe we're sisters?" Rachel asked slowly.

"Oh, yes, I do. Will has a picture of the two of us when we were babies."

"I asked my mother why she had no pictures of me before my third birthday, but she said she couldn't afford the film."

"I think she lied to you, but probably because she loved you and was afraid of losing you. Our parents were killed in a car crash shortly before our third birthday. All of the kids were put up for adoption because we didn't have any other family to take care of us. Wally and Jim, the two oldest, were the only ones not adopted. They went into the foster care system."

"I think my mother has some questions to answer."

"Don't be too hard on her, dear," Vivian said.

"You don't understand, Mrs. Greenfield. I found out last month that she'd spent all my savings I'd been earning since I was fifteen and borrowed against my future earnings. I've worked for ten years and have nothing to show for it, thanks to her. I think she deserves for me to be hard on her."

"Oh, my," Vivian said.

Chapter Thirteen

"What kind of work have you been doing for ten years?" Jeff asked.

"Modeling." She saw their skeptical looks. "Oh, I'm not a high-fashion model. I don't have the cheekbones. I have the 'girl next door' look. I'm in a lot of catalogs and flyers. I made it to the Neiman's Christmas catalog for the first time this year."

"That's very exciting," Vivian said.

"It was. I had quite a savings until my mother started spending it. She said I owed it to her because she never got any child support."

"Have you seen a lawyer?" Jeff asked.

"You expect me to sue my own mother?"

"No, but some well-placed threats might recover whatever she has or could sell."

"Are you a lawyer?"

"Yes."

"Want the job?"

Jeff grinned. "It wouldn't be my favorite job, but I'd do anything for Rebecca's family."

"My, you've made quite a conquest, Rebecca," Rachel said, smiling at Rebecca.

"No, no, you don't understand. Jeff is engaged to be married, but he's also my little boy's father." Rachel's frown made her hasten to add, "He didn't know about Joey until he'd already gotten engaged."

"That sounds bizarre," Rachel said, still staring at Jeff.

"I'll explain later, but if Jeff will try to recover your money, I'd hire him if I were you."

"Then, yes, please, Jeff."

"I'll get your information after lunch."

"I think I'll give my mother a call. I want some answers, and I don't want to wait."

"If you'd like to go into the library, you can be alone, Rachel," Vivian suggested.

"Thank you, Vivian. Could Vanessa and Rebecca come with me?"

"Of course, child. Whatever you want."

The three young women went into the library together.

Jeff looked at Will. "Do you think there's any doubt?"

"No, I don't. But we'll see what her mother says. She'd better get all the information she needs from her mother before the woman finds out you're going to come after her money."

"Can you believe a mother would steal from her own child? I thought Rebecca's parents were no good, but I think even they were better than Rachel's mother."

"It is amazing, isn't it? Who knows what forces motivate a person to behave so poorly—to go out and hurt their children? I can't even begin to understand it," Will said. "Do you think you can recover much of it?"

"It depends. If the woman is driving a new car, has a savings account, has bought some jewelry or furniture, then I can at least get her fifty cents on the dollar. That's better than nothing."

"Yeah. I hope you can help her."

"Dear," Vivian said to Will, "you don't mind if I offer to have her live here, do you? She doesn't have anyone but her mother, and she's not very nice. I'd like her to be here with Vanessa and Rebecca."

"I expected as much, my little den mother," Will said with a grin. "I think that's a great idea."

"Oh, Will, you are so wonderful."

"I think you're both pretty wonderful," Jeff said.

Suddenly the door opened, and the three women came back in.

Rachel was the one to speak. "She lied to me. My family name was Barlow, and Rebecca and I *are* twins. And Vanessa is my baby sister." Her eyes watered but her chin remained firm. "I really can't believe this is happening but I appreciate your looking for me."

Rebecca and Vanessa hugged her. A few of those tears had escaped when she ended that embrace.

"My dear Rachel, we have a spare bedroom. Why don't you come live here with us?"

"Oh, no. I have an apartment. Mostly, I need somewhere my mail can be collected, and a place to stay for a day or two when I come back in town from a shoot.''

"All the more reason you should move in here. Paying rent for a place you don't use doesn't make a lot of sense.''

"I don't want to impose on you.'' Rachel stared when everyone broke into laughter.

Rebecca hugged her again. "Rachel, there's no such thing with Vivian and Will. Did we tell you Vivian's having a baby? We're all so excited. And you'll meet Betty in a minute. That's why they can be so generous. Betty helps take care of all of us.''

"Are you sure?'' Rachel asked, dumbfounded.

"We're sure,'' Vivian said with a gentle smile.

"And I can be your business manager,'' Rebecca said. "I can take your mother's place.''

"I don't even know you, but I'd certainly trust you more than her after all the deception.''

Betty came in to call them to lunch. She hadn't seen the twins together. Earlier she hadn't realized it was Rachel rather than Rebecca. When she entered the room, her mouth open to call them to lunch, she froze, staring at the two girls.

"Betty, I'd like you to meet Rachel, Rebecca's twin.''

"Lordy mercy, they're as alike as two peas in a pod.''

"Yes, they are,'' Will agreed. "Rachel's going to move in here, too, but she won't be here often. She's a model.''

"Well, she's pretty enough. A'course, Rebecca and Vanessa are, too."

"Yes, they are," Rachel agreed. "I could hook them up with some jobs if they're interested."

"I'm in college, attending classes," Vanessa said.

"Me, too. And I couldn't travel and leave Joey." Rebecca gave an apologetic smile to her twin.

"I haven't met Joey yet."

"He comes home from preschool a little later. Peter, Betty's husband, picks him up for me. Usually, I go from class to Jeff's office to work."

"Let's go into lunch," Vivian suggested, leading the way.

They were still lingering over lunch when Joey came home. Betty brought him into the dining room. Both Rebecca and Rachel were sitting on one side of the table, across from Vanessa and Jeff.

"Mommy!" Joey called as he came in, heading for the first twin. Then he caught sight of the second twin. He came to an abrupt halt. "Mommy?"

"I'm Mommy, sweetie," Rebecca said. "This is my twin sister, Rachel."

Joey climbed into his mother's lap and whispered, "She looks just like you."

"I know. That's what being twins means."

"Oh. But how do I tell you apart?"

"I'll always tell you which one is me."

"Okay." He raised his head and looked at Rachel. "Hello."

"Hello, Joey. I'm delighted to meet you."

Instead of answering Rachel, Joey smiled at his mother. "Her voice is different from yours."

"Yes, it is."

"Good."

Jeff, having made the same observation, smiled at his son. It had relieved his mind, too.

After lunch, Jeff asked Rachel questions about her mother's finances. Then he went back to the office, telling Rebecca she didn't need to come to work that afternoon.

"Generous boss," Rachel said, elbowing Rebecca in a friendly manner.

"Yes, he is. Want to go pack up your apartment this afternoon?"

"I don't think we can do it in one afternoon."

"Then we'd definitely better get started. When's your next job?"

"I leave Friday for the Caribbean."

"Wow, you're lucky," Vanessa said.

"Yeah, but I don't get to look around or tour the islands at all. And after posing in swimsuits for five or six hours on the beach, I don't want to spend any more time there."

"I can understand that," Rebecca said, "but I'm not a beach person."

"I am," Vanessa said, "but you're probably right. That would be too many hours on the beach. I like to shower and get the sand out of my mouth." She turned to her mother. "Mom, do you mind if I go help Rachel and Rebecca pack up her apartment?"

"No, of course not, dear. Who will be home for dinner?"

Rebecca looked at Rachel and then Vanessa. "I think we all will be. After packing all afternoon, we'll probably have huge appetites."

"I'll tell Betty," Vivian said with a laugh.

"Not on my account. I can't put on any weight before a shoot."

"There's another reason I don't want to be a model," Vanessa said. "I don't want anything to mess with my appetite."

Chuckling, the three young women linked arms and headed for the front door.

IT WAS A BUSY WEEK at the law office. In addition to his regular clients, Jeff worked on Rachel's situation, which involved an ugly interview with her adoptive mother. The woman was a selfish, not-too-bright person.

Jeff had used veiled threats, but unfortunately he didn't think there would be a lot he could reclaim on Rachel's behalf. Still, he intended to do the best he could.

On Thursday, toward the end of the day, Bill came into his office. "Have you talked to Chelsea this week?"

"Chelsea?" Jeff asked, his mind still on other things.

"Yeah, you remember her, your fiancée?" Bill said in a sarcastic tone.

"Sorry. My mind was on a case. No, I haven't talked to Chelsea this week. It's been sort of hectic."

"Yeah, especially with Rebecca not working this week." Bill paused before adding, "I'm going to have to hire a secretary, even when Rebecca returns to work."

"Yeah. I'm sure she'll be back next week. But you're right about needing to hire someone. You might ask Harriet if she knows a good prospect."

"Good idea. Um, could you try to call Chelsea?"

Jeff stared at Bill. "Try? You make it sound like you don't think I can."

"Well, I've tried several times, but her mother always says she's indisposed at the moment and offers to take a message."

Jeff frowned. Then he picked up the phone and dialed Chelsea's number. Just as Bill had predicted, the phone was answered by Chelsea's mother.

"Mrs. Wexham, this is Jeff. Is Chelsea around?"

"I'm afraid she's not feeling well, Jeff. May I take a message?"

"Sure. Can you please tell her to call me. Has she seen a doctor?"

"No, it's not that serious. I'm sure she'll feel better in a few days."

"If it affects her that long, shouldn't she see a doctor?"

"Jeff, I'm her mother. I know what's best for my daughter. She'll return your call when she can."

Jeff put down the phone, still frowning.

"Killer Mom, right?"

"Yeah. When did you first call?"

"Monday afternoon. I thought I'd tell her about Rebecca's twin. I thought she'd want to know. She and Rebecca have grown pretty close."

"Yeah. So if anyone can breach the mother's guard, it would be Rebecca." He picked up the phone again and dialed from memory. "Betty, is Rebecca there? Oh, good. May I speak with her?"

He stood there waiting, the tapping of his foot the only indication he was impatient. "Becca, could you do me a favor? Can you please try calling Chelsea. Both Bill and I have tried, and her mother makes excuses about why she can't come to the phone. She says Chelsea isn't feeling well, but she hasn't gone to a doctor."

He paused, then said, "Thanks. Let me know what happens. I'll wait for your call." Then he hung up the phone. He turned and looked at Bill. "Rebecca is going to try to get through to her."

"Mind if I wait with you?" Bill asked.

"No, I don't mind." Jeff gestured to an empty chair. "Make yourself comfortable." He sat down behind his desk and began working.

Bill opened his mouth, as if to speak. He closed it again and sat down in one of the leather chairs in front of Jeff's desk. Then he got up again, unable to sit still. "I think I'll go talk to Harriet about a secretary."

"Good idea. I'll let you know what Rebecca says."

"Yeah. I appreciate it."

Jeff's phone rang a few minutes later. "Jacobs," he said, hoping it was Rebecca.

"Jeff, I spoke to Chelsea. I'm going over to see her."

"Why?"

"She's not feeling well, and none of us have checked on her. I think she feels neglected."

"Bill said he tried to call her several times, and her mother wouldn't let him talk to her."

"Probably true, but Bill isn't her fiancé."

Oooh. The dig hurt. "Becca—"

"I have to go."

Before he could say anything else, he heard the dial tone, meaning she'd gone. Then he looked up and saw Bill staring at him from the doorway. "Rebecca talked to her. Now she's going over to visit her. Said she thinks Chelsea feels I've neglected her."

Bill frowned. "But why wouldn't she take my calls?"

"I don't know. I tried to ask Rebecca some questions, but she hung up before I could."

"I should go over there. If she's feeling well enough to see Rebecca, she should be able to see me," Bill said.

"Because you're…" Jeff paused, waiting for Bill to complete the sentence.

Bill met his gaze. "Because I'm her friend."

"I think we'd both better wait for Rebecca to call back."

REBECCA PARKED IN FRONT of the Wexham home and picked up the box of chocolates she'd bought for

Chelsea. She felt like she should've dressed in velvet to visit the Wexhams, or at least silk.

After ringing the doorbell, she stood waiting for it to open. When it did, a gray-haired woman in a maid's uniform stared at her.

"Hello. I'm Rebecca Barlow. I'm here to see Chelsea."

"I'm not sure—"

"I talked to Chelsea a few moments ago and she invited me over."

"Oh. Then I guess you can come in." She backed away from the door.

With a smile, Rebecca passed her. "Is her room upstairs?"

"Yes, ma'am. Second door on the right."

"Thank you." Rebecca started up the stairs. Chelsea had said her mother would be gone for an hour to a meeting, which made it possible for Rebecca to get in to see her. Much to Rebecca's amazement, Chelsea's mother had been holding her daughter prisoner.

She knocked on the door. "Chelsea?"

Chelsea opened the door and invited her into a beautiful bedroom.

"Oh, your room is lovely, Chelsea. Did you decorate it yourself?" Rebecca said, noting the difference between this room and the rest of the house she'd seen. "It's so warm and inviting."

"Yes, I did my room myself. It was my twenty-first birthday gift from my dad. My mother hates it."

"How are you feeling?"

"I'm fine. I was more confused than sick."

After drawing a deep breath, Rebecca offered the chocolates. "I thought these might raise your spirits."

"How did you know these were my favorites?" Chelsea asked as she opened the box and selected a piece of chocolate. Then she offered the chocolates to Rebecca.

Rebecca took a piece and bit into it, as did Chelsea. As they chewed in silent companionship, Rebecca said softly, "What were you confused about?"

"Oh, life, I guess. Maybe my engagement. That's what upset Mother. She had great plans for me after my marriage. She felt with my social connections through Jeff, I could soon become president of Junior League. She was upset that I showed no interest in that future."

"What if—what if Joey and I moved away? Would that help clear things up?" That comment came out of the blue and Rebecca wasn't exactly keen on the idea, but she immediately knew it was what she had to do. She couldn't handle being around Jeff constantly if he married Chelsea. And she didn't want to be responsible for breaking up their engagement.

"Why would you do that, Rebecca? I thought you and Joey were very happy here."

"We are. But that doesn't mean we couldn't be happy somewhere else. If we moved, to, say, Oklahoma City, we'd be close enough to visit occasionally, but not so close that we'd be in everyone's lives every minute of every day."

Chelsea stared at her, saying nothing.

"I know it's been difficult for you since Jeff found out about Joey. He's so focused on Joey, which includes me, ever since he found out."

"Yes, but—"

"You've been more than patient and understanding, Chelsea. But if you'll just give me a couple of days more, we'll be out of your hair."

"You would do that? You would completely uproot your lives just to make things easier for me?"

"And Jeff. You both had a future planned before we burst into your lives."

"Rebecca, I don't think—"

"It's all right, Chelsea. I've known for a while that life was becoming too difficult for you. I tried to warn Jeff, but he couldn't see it. But I'll take care of everything. Just be patient."

"No, Rebecca—"

But Rebecca didn't wait for any more conversation. She kissed Chelsea's cheek and hurried out of the house.

Leaving Chelsea even more confused than ever.

REBECCA FELT AS IF SHE'D understood Chelsea's confusion. She wasn't prepared to be a stepmother. But even more, it must have hurt her every time Jeff had shoved her aside for Rebecca and Joey.

It had hurt Rebecca, too. Because she'd wanted to be beside Jeff, to be important to him, but not at Chelsea's expense. She'd been letting Jeff place her in an impossible position.

Now she was going to do what was right and fair. It wouldn't be easy. That much she already knew. But the pain was her own fault. Well, not the pain of leaving Vanessa and Rachel, Will and Vivian. But the pain of leaving Jeff was her fault.

She decided the easiest way would be to do what she had to do and not leave anyone the time to argue her out of it. When she got back to her room, she pulled out the trust papers she'd signed. She thought she'd remembered Will saying she had the right to withdraw the money whenever she wanted.

Carefully making a list of what she must do before leaving, she planned her and Joey's escape for early Saturday morning. If they got away by nine o'clock, they could be in Oklahoma City by one o'clock. They could have lunch there, find a hotel and then start looking for a place to live. And with Jeff's money, they could afford to rent a two-bedroom apartment, which would be much nicer than what they'd had in Little Rock.

Then she would find a day care for Joey and a job for herself, and they would be all set. And lonely. But they would survive, and they could come visit their family once every two or three months.

Then they wouldn't be a burden to anyone, or interfere in other people's lives. She fought back a sob just as the phone rang. She didn't answer it, knowing Betty would do so. She was afraid she knew who was calling.

With a deep breath, she tried to sound normal when

she picked up the phone after Betty had called up the stairs to her.

"Hello?"

"Becca, it's Jeff. You didn't call back."

"Oh, I'm sorry. I forgot. Chelsea just has a slight cold. Another day or two in bed and I'm sure she'll be feeling fine. I took her some chocolates and told her we were missing her. It seemed to cheer her up."

"But why isn't she taking any phone calls?" Jeff asked, puzzlement in his voice.

"Because her mother has convinced her that she shouldn't talk to anyone or appear in public until she's at her best. You know her mother."

"Yeah, I guess I do. Well, thanks for checking on her. How are you and Joey doing? I've missed you two this week, too."

"Joey's missed you, too. But we've been busy. Were you able to do any good with Rachel's mother?"

"I'm working on it. She's not an easy woman to deal with."

"Well, no, she doesn't sound like a wonderful person, stealing from her child."

"She even makes your parents sound good."

"Yes, she does."

"So when can I see you and Joey again?"

"Why don't you come over for dinner tonight?"

"I'd love to. I'll be there by six-thirty."

Rebecca hung up the phone feeling terribly guilty. She'd asked Jeff over without checking with either Vivian or Betty first. But that was the least of her sins.

Chapter Fourteen

Rebecca hurried down the stairs to tell Betty that she'd invited Jeff for dinner and was fully prepared to apologize profusely.

But rather than chastise her, Betty was excited. "Oh, good. I baked some coconut cream pies for dessert tonight. I think he'll really like them."

Rebecca almost burst into tears. Then she hugged Betty and promised to help in any way she could.

"Don't be silly, child. We're having roast beef tonight. It's been cooking for a couple of hours already. The vegetable dishes are already prepared. I'm baking frozen rolls that I've had rising for an hour and dessert is already made. All I have to do is set the table, and if you do that, I'll have nothing to do."

Rebecca hugged Betty again. Then she went searching for Vivian to confess her dastardly deed. She found her in the library, writing a letter.

"Vivian, I invited Jeff for dinner tonight without asking you first. I apologize—"

"That's nice, dear. Is Rachel coming for dinner as well?"

"Yes, she is. Oh, I forgot to remind Betty that Rachel's coming." She whirled to head back to the kitchen, but Vivian stopped her.

"She knows Rachel would probably be here. When will she actually move in with us?"

"Today," Rebecca said, not realizing until that moment that her twin would be moving in two days before she planned to move out.

Vivian looked at Rebecca sharply. "You're okay with her moving in, aren't you?"

"Oh, yes. I think it was terribly kind of you to invite her to stay here. I think she was feeling very much alone after her mother's betrayal."

"Yes, I suppose she was. Just as you had felt alone after your parents' rejection of you and Joey."

"Yes. I don't know if I've ever told you how much your welcoming arms meant to us. Joey has become a different little boy from your and Will's acceptance of him."

"I feel sorry for your parents, Rebecca. If you want to invite them for a weekend, I could put them up in a hotel. You could let them get to know Joey. Maybe that would change them."

"No, Vivian. I won't do that. I contacted my mother several times after Joey's birth, inviting her to lunch so she could meet Joey. She refused every time because she was afraid my father would find out."

"I know, dear. But it's hard to live under someone's thumb and make the right decisions. I know, because Vanessa's father was that kind of man."

"I don't think he was as bad as my father."

"Maybe not as bad, but only because I fought him on many subjects."

"My mother had no courage. And I won't invite that man to meet Joey. My worst fear would be that he *would* like Joey and would try to mold him after him."

"Perhaps you're right, dear. All I can say is that we are the lucky ones since we have you and Joey in our lives."

Rebecca burst into tears. Vivian immediately rose and put her arms around Rebecca. "Child, why should that make you cry?"

Rebecca shook her head, unable to explain. Finally, she lifted her head and wiped her eyes. "It's just that you and Will are the kindest, nicest people on the earth, and yet you say you're the lucky ones."

"That's no reason to cry. I think you've been taking on the stress in everyone's lives lately. You need to get more rest this evening."

"Yes, yes, I will. I'm sorry, Vivian."

"Stop apologizing, child."

"But you're the one who should be crying. You're pregnant."

"Oh, no. That's something to celebrate."

"You're right, of course, but that didn't stop me from crying when I was pregnant."

"Yes, but you were alone, Rebecca, and I'm surrounded by loved ones. That makes a big difference. Family makes all the difference in the world. That's why I had Will start this search for your siblings."

"I'm glad. I guess I'd better go tell Joey his daddy

is coming to dinner. That will encourage him to get cleaned up.''

Rebecca slipped out of the library, regretting her burst of tears. She didn't want to give Vivian any reason to think anything was wrong. She knew she was doing the right thing. She'd realized Jeff couldn't continue to put Chelsea third in his life without there being repercussions. But he hadn't listened to her.

So she would have to be the one to make everything right. It wouldn't be that hard on Joey. He would know his daddy loved him and he would get to spend time with him every once in a while. And Rebecca would bring him to see Will and Vivian and Rachel and Vanessa when she could.

It would be all right. She kept repeating that to herself all afternoon as she packed one of their big suitcases. When Joey came in and caught her, he wanted to know what she was doing.

''I'm storing away your summer clothes. The suitcase is a good place to keep them until it gets hot again. That won't be for a long time, you know.''

''I know. We're learning about winter at school. Did you know that in some places, they have snow all the time?''

''Yes, I did know that, Joey. I'm glad you're learning so much.''

''It doesn't snow here much.''

''No, I've heard it doesn't. But it does get cold. You can't wear short pants in the winter.''

''That's okay. I like wearing jeans.''

"Good. We probably need to buy you another couple of pairs."

"Daddy said he would buy me some clothes. Maybe I'll ask him for more jeans."

"No!" Rebecca realized she'd spoken too sharply. "It's just that your daddy is putting away money for your college education, and that takes a lot of money. So he's paying more than his share. And he's giving me money every month to take care of you. So I'll buy you more jeans."

"Okay. Is everything okay, Mommy?"

Rebecca quickly hugged her child. "Yes, of course, sweetie. Everything's fine."

She hurriedly put the suitcase under her bed as soon as Joey had left the room. It was almost time for Rachel and Vanessa to come home, and she doubted either of them would have accepted her explanation. If she had to confess her departure this far in advance, she would never be able to get away. She knew she wasn't strong enough to withstand the persuasions of her family.

WILL STOPPED BY JEFF'S OFFICE that afternoon to ask him a question about his work. As they finished talking, Will suggested he come to dinner that evening.

"Actually, I am coming. Rebecca invited me this afternoon."

"Oh, good. Oh, hello, Bill. How are you settling in?" Will asked as they ran into Bill as Will was leaving.

"Pretty well."

"Say, Jeff's coming to dinner this evening. Why don't you come, too? I always hated eating alone when I was single."

"Are you sure it won't be too many people?"

"I'm sure. Vivian loves meals with lots of guests."

"Then I'd love to join you."

Jeff nodded as Will turned to say goodbye, thanking him for his invitation to Bill. Jeff had intended to offer to have dinner with Bill, but he couldn't turn down an invitation from Rebecca. He'd tried to explain Chelsea's deal about her mother, but Bill was having trouble grasping how a strong-willed woman could run roughshod over her entire family.

Bill hadn't met Mrs. Wexham.

"You think it's okay that I accepted, don't you?" Bill asked.

"Of course it is. Will wouldn't have asked if he hadn't wanted you to come. I told you they were nice people."

"Yeah. You never say that about Chelsea's parents."

"No, I don't." He smiled at Bill and retreated to his office.

Just before he got ready to leave the office, shortly after six, his phone rang. He answered since Harriet had long gone home. "Jacobs."

"Jeff, it's Chelsea."

"Well, hi, there. You sound good. Your cold must be getting better."

"Uh, yes. Have you talked to Rebecca since she came to see me today?"

"Yes, I have. In fact, I'm going to have dinner with all of them in a few minutes. Bill's going with me, too. By the way, you should call him. He's been very worried about you."

"Yes, but—did Rebecca sound okay?"

"Yeah, she sounded fine. Why?"

"I—I just wondered."

"What made you think—"

"I have to go now."

And he again heard the dial tone in his ear. He appeared to have a strange effect on the women in his life. But why had Chelsea thought something was wrong with Rebecca?

He stopped by Bill's office to let him know he was ready.

"Chelsea just called."

Bill's head snapped up. "She did? How did she sound?"

"Just fine. She called to see if I'd talked to Rebecca since she'd visited her."

"Why?"

"I don't know. She apparently thought she'd been upset. But I talked to Rebecca, and she sounded fine to me."

"Did you tell Chelsea I'd been trying to call her?"

"Yes, and I told her that she should call you. But I also told her you were going to dinner with me at the Greenfields', so she probably won't try until later."

"I see. Maybe I'll try her after dinner."

"She might be going to bed early tonight, to make

sure she's over her cold. Why don't you call her to-morrow?''

''Yeah, that might be best.''

In Jeff's car on the drive to dinner, Bill seemed almost jittery to Jeff. ''Is anything wrong, Bill? Are you unhappy with our business arrangement?''

''No, everything's fine. And Harriet is having a friend come in to interview for the secretary job. The woman is working as a legal secretary now, but she's very unhappy with the law office she's currently working for.''

''That sounds promising, unless she's one of those people who are usually unhappy.''

''I think Harriet would know it if she were one of those kind of people.''

''You're probably right. You'll know when you interview her.''

''Yeah.''

Jeff parked the car in front of Vivian and Will's house, and before either man could get out of the car, the front door opened and Joey came running toward them.

''Now, there's a welcome every man should get,'' Bill murmured.

Jeff hurried out of the car and met his son with his arms open. He swung him up into his arms for a big hug.

Then Bill asked for a hug, too. Joey willingly gave him one, but he remained in his father's arms.

''Does your mommy know you were coming out

to meet me?'' Jeff asked as Rebecca appeared in the doorway Joey had left open.

Joey shook his head, a guilty look on his face.

''Then I think we've got some explaining to do,'' Jeff said.

''Hi, Mommy,'' Joey said, fear in his voice.

''Stop acting like I'm going to beat you, young man,'' Rebecca said. ''But you shouldn't leave the door open, and you shouldn't leave the house without telling an adult.''

''But, Mommy—''

''Yes, ma'am, Mommy,'' Jeff said insistently.

''Yes, ma'am, Mommy,'' Joey repeated. Then he turned to his father. ''What's 'ma'am' mean?''

They all burst out laughing.

Bill supplied the answer. ''That's a polite way to address ladies.''

''Oh. So I should call my teacher, ma'am?'' Joey asked.

''You could, but probably you should just call her by her name. Mrs. whatever her name is.'' Jeff smiled to accompany his words.

''Mrs. Peabody,'' Joey supplied.

''Well, I think Mrs. Peabody would prefer that you call her Mrs. Peabody instead of ma'am.''

''Mommy likes me to call her Mommy, don't you, Mommy?''

''Yes, sweetie, I do. But it's good to know polite words in case you're talking to another lady.''

''Okay.'' He wiggled out of his dad's arms when

they reached the house. "I'll go tell Betty you're here."

After the boy disappeared, Jeff said, "Thanks for helping me out of that conversation."

Bill laughed. "I was hoping it would continue. It's not often I see Jeff bested in a conversation."

Rebecca smiled, but she didn't laugh.

"Are you feeling okay?" Jeff asked, thinking again about Chelsea's phone call.

"Yes, fine. This week with Rachel coming into our lives has been wonderful but a little bit stressful, you know, adjusting," Rebecca said.

"But you're getting along all right, aren't you?" Bill asked in surprise.

"Oh, yes, of course, but it's amazing how often we know what each other is thinking." She was worried about that. Rachel would leave tomorrow morning and be gone for a couple of weeks. If she could hide her turmoil from Rachel until the morning, she could manage to pull off her departure.

"I guess that would be hard to adjust to," Bill said.

"Yeah," Jeff agreed belatedly. "I'm not sure I'd like it."

Rebecca didn't want to continue to discuss her relationship with her twin. "I think Will is waiting for us in the library. And I'm sure Betty will be bringing in hors d'oeuvres soon."

She smiled and waved them into the house.

After the two men reached the library, Bill whispered, "That's the second time Rebecca bested you in a conversation. She's dangerous."

"Yeah, I know." Jeff shook hands with Will and sat down. "Will, have you talked to Rebecca today?"

"Um, I think I spoke to her at breakfast. I'm not at my best early in the morning."

"No, I mean this afternoon. She just showed us in here and disappeared."

Vivian entered at that moment. All the men greeted her. Then Will asked, "Is Rebecca doing all right?"

"Why do you ask?" Vivian stared at her husband with wide eyes.

"Jeff was wondering if everything is all right. Rebecca showed him and Bill in here and then disappeared."

"Perhaps she wasn't quite ready for guests. I'm sure she'll be down soon." With a smile, Vivian sat down beside Bill. "We're so glad you could join us this evening, Bill."

"Thank you, Mrs. Greenfield. I'm looking forward to a home-cooked meal."

"Call me Vivian, Bill. And that's Will. Right, dear?"

"Definitely Will," Will agreed with a grin. "Vivian rules the roost around here, Bill, so you may as well give in."

The door opened again and three young ladies entered.

"Oh, Rachel and Vanessa, you're back," Vivian greeted them.

"Bill and Jeff are joining us for dinner. And Rebecca, they were concerned that you hadn't joined us yet."

"I'm sorry. I hadn't finished fixing my hair when I ran after Joey. I thought I'd take a minute to get the hair out of my eyes."

"And you look lovely. All three of you do. Rachel, have you got all your things moved in?"

"Yes, Vivian, we finished this afternoon. Vanessa helped me."

"Oh, good. I'm glad you're finally here."

Betty entered with a tray of hors d'oeuvres. "Here now, this should hold you until dinner is ready."

"Thank you, Betty. I'm sure it will," Vivian agreed.

After Betty had left the room, Bill said, "This could hold me until Saturday."

Will chuckled. "I know, but you have to share with us."

"Oh, I knew there was a catch." Bill got up and passed the tray around.

A few minutes later, Betty called them in to dinner. She served the roast beef and vegetables, then said, before leaving the room, "Be sure you save room for dessert. I baked coconut cream pies."

Rachel groaned after Betty left the room. "I knew moving in here was a mistake. I can't stay on a diet around here."

"Yes, you can, dear," Vivian promised. "I'll make sure she adds some lower-calorie vegetables and not as many good desserts."

"Oh, no, I won't be here often enough to make everyone hate me. And *I* would hate me if I changed Betty's menu."

"Good for you," Will said. "I enjoy every calorie I eat of Betty's cooking. It's why I keep working out in the gym."

"I try to do some kind of physical regime, but with all the traveling I do, it isn't easy. And then I meet Rebecca, who looks just like me, and she doesn't diet at all."

"Ah, Joey's my secret. Keeping up with him is my workout." Rebecca smiled at her son. He was seated between her and Jeff. Vanessa and Rachel sat on the other side with Bill.

When dinner was over, it was almost Joey's bedtime. Everyone retired to the library, but Rebecca told Joey to tell everyone good-night. He did so, but Jeff immediately stood and offered to help put him to bed.

Rebecca hesitated. She wanted to refuse his offer, but she couldn't do that. It might be the last time Jeff tucked Joey in for a long time.

Jeff carried his son upstairs and helped him brush his teeth and don his pajamas in the bathroom. They came into Joey's bedroom, both laughing.

"What's so funny?" Rebecca asked.

"Joey was making funny faces in the mirror."

"You started it, Daddy," Joey said.

Jeff laughed. "I guess I did."

"Choose the book you want us to read, but not the dinosaur book."

"Why not?" Jeff asked.

"Because it's his longest book. That's why he chooses it so often."

"Aw, Mommy."

She crossed her arms and stared at her son. With a shrug of his shoulder, Joey picked another book about a dog.

"Someday I want to have a dog," he said as he gave it to his father.

"Maybe someday you can. What kind would you like?"

"I like golden retrievers."

"Those dogs are bigger than you are," Jeff protested.

"But I'm going to grow, aren't I?"

"Yes, you are, son. And I'm going to watch you grow."

Rebecca turned her back to the pair. She was afraid her face would give away her anguish.

"Rebecca? You ready to read?"

"You start. I want to tidy up the bathroom."

When she came back into the room a couple of minutes later, Jeff was halfway through the book. She took over the reading for the last few pages. Then she kissed her son good-night and stood, waiting for Jeff to do the same.

When he'd done so, she tucked the covers around her little boy, kissed him again and tiptoed to the door where Jeff waited.

"Are you okay?" Jeff asked when they had closed Joey's door.

"Yes, of course, why?"

"I just got the feeling you were upset."

"Please, I don't need anyone else reading my mind." She hurried down the stairs ahead of Jeff.

Betty was bringing in a tray of coffee and hot tea when they reached the library. Jeff gave a sigh. ''I think coffee is the perfect antidote to that pie.''

''But, Mr. Jeff, I thought you'd want an extra piece to take home,'' Betty said, a shocked look on her face.

Jeff began to stammer, trying to think of a way to avoid hurting Betty's feelings.

''He's afraid he'll put on weight and Chelsea won't want him anymore.'' Rebecca finished by smiling at Jeff, but it wasn't a pleasant smile.

Jeff gave his apologies to Betty. Then he accepted his fragrant cup of coffee.

After an enjoyable hour, the two men excused themselves. As they walked to the car, Bill commented on the pleasant evening and got almost no response from Jeff.

''Is something wrong?''

''Yeah, I'm beginning to think Chelsea was right. There's something wrong with Rebecca.''

Chapter Fifteen

Friday morning, Rebecca got Joey off to school. Then she joined Vivian, Vanessa and Rachel at the breakfast table. Rachel would have to leave soon to make her flight. Peter was going to drive her as soon as he got back from taking Joey to school.

"In honor of your departure, Rachel, I think I'll have just one more cinnamon roll. These are even better than the coconut pie last night," Rebecca said, closing her eyes to savor the taste.

"Yes, they are," Rachel agreed.

Rebecca's eyes popped open. "Did you eat one?"

"No. But Vanessa gave me a bite of hers."

"I'm glad you ate your scrambled eggs, Rachel," Vivian said. "They have a lot of protein in them."

"Yes. Eggs are one of my favorite foods." Rachel paused before she said, "Eggs and cinnamon rolls."

They all laughed. Betty came in and poured more coffee in Rachel's cup.

"Thank you, Betty." After Betty went back to the kitchen, Rachel said, "I'm going to miss this service while I'm gone. It seems like all they do is yell at us at these shoots.''

"That doesn't sound pleasant," Vivian said with a frown.

"It's not. Modeling is not an easy job, but it pays well. If it weren't for Mother stealing all my money, I'd have a nice nest egg."

"How much had you saved?" Vanessa asked.

"Almost seventy-five thousand. And that included paying Mother a salary to handle my money."

"Your mother spent that much money?" Rebecca asked.

"Yes, over a period of a year. And borrowed another twenty-five thousand against my future earnings."

"Oh, my," Vivian said, her gaze sad. "That woman has no right to call herself your mother."

"Certainly not compared to you, Vivian," Rachel said with a smile. "Now, I've got to go. I hear Peter in the driveway and he said we'd have to hurry."

She hugged all three women goodbye. "This is the first time I've gone on a shoot and really had family to say goodbye to." She brushed away the tears, grabbed the suitcase she'd brought down with her and ran out the door.

Rebecca gave a sigh of relief.

"You're glad she's gone?" Vivian asked, staring at her.

"I'm glad the goodbyes are over. I'm not very good at them. And I knew they might be difficult this morning." Rebecca breathed a sigh of relief when she saw understanding in Vivian's smile and gaze. She stood, excusing herself.

"I guess you do have to go so you won't be late to class."

Rebecca had intended to tell them she wasn't going to school today because she had too much to do, but she couldn't do that. So she grabbed her purse and books to hurry out. Only she didn't go to class. Instead, she went to the library. There she wrote goodbye letters to Will and Vivian, Rachel, Vanessa and Jeff.

She received several funny stares as she wrote while tears slid down her cheeks. She kept a tissue in her hand and mopped them up, but the tears kept coming.

"Rebecca?"

Rebecca gasped as she realized Vanessa had come to the library and found her. "Vanessa!" she managed to get out.

"What's wrong?" Vanessa whispered as she slipped into the chair beside her. "And why aren't you in class?"

"I couldn't go. I was too upset."

"Because Rachel left?"

"Yes, it seemed to release some emotions I hadn't dealt with. I'm sorry. I thought if I wrote about them I'd feel better."

"It doesn't seem to be working. Why don't we go get a hamburger together?"

"Okay, that's a good idea." Rebecca quickly

tucked her letters away so her sister couldn't see them.

They walked a short distance to a favorite lunch place the students enjoyed. They found a table, and Vanessa insisted Rebecca sit down while she went and got their food. Rebecca could only agree.

Vanessa came back to their table with a tray full of food. "I got us some onion rings, too. I never asked you if you like them, but since we seem to like all the same things I thought you might like them, too."

"You noticed that about all of us?"

Vanessa grinned and nodded.

"Well, you're right. I love onion rings. I don't think I can eat all this food, though, after those cinnamon rolls for breakfast."

"It's a good thing Rachel won't be going on a trip every morning. We'd all get fat."

"Yes." Rebecca took the thick hamburger off the tray, cheese dripping down its sides. "Oh, this looks so good."

"I know. I love these hamburgers. It took me a while to convince Betty that college kids didn't take sack lunches to school."

"No—really?"

"Really. She'd always packed lunches for me because she was sure that the school food would be bad for me." Vanessa grinned as Rebecca laughed.

"It sounds good to hear you laugh, Rebecca. I was afraid you were falling to pieces back there in the library."

"No, I'm fine. It was just a hard day."

"Are you going in to work today?"

"No. I've missed all week. I don't see that going in today would do any good." She released her breath as Vanessa nodded in agreement.

"True. Have you told Jeff?"

"No, I thought I'd give him a call in a few minutes."

"Here, you can use my cell phone and call him now."

Vivian had wanted to get Rebecca a cell phone, but she'd refused. She didn't consider one essential. "All right, if you're sure you don't mind."

"Of course not."

Rebecca dialed the number for the law office. When Harriet answered, she began giving her the message for Jeff.

"Jeff specifically said if you called I was to let him know so he could talk to you. Just a minute."

Rebecca wanted to protest, but Harriet had already gotten up and wasn't there to hear her words.

"Is anything wrong?" Vanessa asked.

Rebecca shook her head no.

"Rebecca?" Jeff's strong voice sounded in her ear.

"Yes, Jeff?"

"You're not coming in to work today?"

"I didn't think one more day would matter since I've missed all week."

"No, that's fine if you don't want to come in. Are you all right?"

"I'm fine."

"I was thinking about taking Joey shopping tomorrow to buy him some winter clothes. We can have lunch out, too. Is that okay with you?"

"No, tomorrow's not convenient. Maybe next weekend."

"What have you got planned for Saturday?"

"We're way behind on several chores, and I want us to get caught up on them."

"Can I help?"

"No, you can't."

"But I haven't seen much of you…and Joey this week."

"Jeff, don't be difficult. You came to dinner last night."

"Okay. You're sure nothing's wrong?"

"I'm sure."

"Okay. I'll see you Sunday."

He waited, as if to see if she would protest.

She didn't bother. "Goodbye."

"Bye."

"Why was he being difficult?" Vanessa asked.

"He wanted to see Joey on Saturday, but I didn't want to spend the day with him."

"Why didn't you let him take Joey for the day? You could have some rest."

"The invitation was for both of us."

"It's a wonder Chelsea doesn't get jealous."

"She does. And I feel terrible about it."

"Oh, I'm sorry."

"Yes. I didn't think I'd like her, but I do. I've tried to tell Jeff he can't put me and Joey first and always leave Chelsea as third, or she would become resentful. I also told him that he had to stop turning her over to Bill's care. But Jeff acts like there's no problem.'' Tears had filled Rebecca's eyes, and she tried to blink them away.

''Is that one of the reasons you were crying in the library?''

''Yes, I'm afraid so.''

''Well, I imagine Chelsea will let him know that.''

Rebecca was so tempted to tell her sister about her conversation with Chelsea, but she couldn't or Vanessa would know what she planned to do and try to stop her. She would tell her parents, and Rebecca knew she wasn't strong enough to stand up to their persuasions.

''Probably so.''

''MRS. WEXHAM, I NEED TO speak to Chelsea. It's an emergency,'' Jeff said.

''What kind of emergency?''

''It's *my* emergency. Either you let me speak to her, or I'm coming over to talk to her in person.''

''That's not possible. She's in her bedroom.''

Jeff hung up the phone, then started out of the office. Then he went back to Bill's office door. ''I'm going to force my way through Mrs. Wexham's fortress. Want to come?''

''Sure. Why are you going to do this?''

''Because something is wrong with Rebecca, and I think Chelsea knows more than she's told me about it. The dragon lady won't let me talk to Chelsea on the phone, so I'm going to demand to see her in person.''

''Sounds like a good idea. We can surround her.''

''I'll take all the help I can get.''

After they got in the car, Jeff said, ''I think it might help the situation if I introduce you as the senator's son. Would you mind too much?''

''If you think it will help, I won't hide in the bushes.''

''Thanks, Bill. You're a good friend.''

Bill didn't respond.

They parked in front of the house. Just as they got out of their car, Chelsea's father pulled into the driveway in his Mercedes.

''Do you think she sent for reinforcements?''

''I find that hard to believe,'' Jeff said. He'd always figured Mrs. Wexham ruled the house.

As they walked to the front door, Mr. Wexham came around to meet them. ''Jeff, what are you doing here?''

''I need to speak with Chelsea, and for a week your wife has given me excuse after excuse about why Chelsea can't come to the phone.''

''Didn't you try her cell phone?''

''There's been no answer on her cell phone for four days.''

''Really? Has she been sick?''

''I was told she had a cold.''

''Really? Well, come on in. We need to get to the bottom of this.''

''Sir, have you met my law partner?''

"No, I don't think I have," the man said as the door opened.

Jeff checked to be sure Mrs. Wexham could hear him. "This is Bill Wallace. His dad is Robert Wallace, one of our senators."

"To the U.S. Congress? Really? Well, welcome, young man."

Jeff saw Mrs. Wexham's eyes widen in surprise, and then narrow in speculation.

"Mrs. Wexham, I'm sorry to interrupt your day, but I need to speak with Chelsea."

"I'll go get her," Mrs. Wexham said with a smile, her gaze fixed on Bill.

Jeff felt sure he knew the conversation that would take place upstairs. Chelsea was about to get chewed out for not telling her mother what she didn't know. She was about to be surprised.

When Mrs. Wexham and Chelsea entered the room a few minutes later, Jeff thought he saw confirmation in Chelsea's gaze. She was furious with Bill.

"Chelsea, I wonder if I could have a few minutes in private with you?" Jeff asked.

Abruptly, Chelsea stopped glaring at Bill and stared at Jeff. "With me? Yes, I suppose so."

As they left the room, Jeff could hear Mrs. Wexham starting the cross-examination. It wouldn't be long before she learned about the oil wells the family owned, too. Then Bill would find the door wide open should he ever want to visit.

"Chelsea, why did you call me to ask if Rebecca was okay yesterday?"

"She talked strangely while she was here."

"About what?"

"About leaving."

Jeff grabbed her shoulders and shouted, "What? What did she say?"

"Jeff, don't do that, you're hurting me."

Bill suddenly appeared in the doorway. "Jeff! What are you doing to Chelsea?"

"Nothing! I mean, I may have squeezed too tightly on her shoulders, but she told me Rebecca is planning on leaving."

"Leaving? Why would she go?"

"She—she was worried about us."

"Us who?" Bill asked.

Chelsea drew back, but bravely said, "Me and Jeff."

"Oh, I see. I'll wait outside, Jeff."

As he turned to leave, Chelsea called, "Bill, don't go."

"Why should I stay? This is between you and your fiancé."

"No, he's not my fiancé anymore. At least not for long. Not in my heart, anyway. That's why Mother was so mad and took away my cell phone, my car keys, and threatened me," Chelsea said.

"What do you mean you're not engaged anymore? And besides, you could have come to me. All you had to do was call," Bill assured her lovingly.

"Oh, really? Well, all you had to do was tell me your father is a senator, and I wouldn't have had any problems. Unless you're lying?"

"No, I'm not lying."

"Why didn't you tell me?"

"Because that wasn't why I wanted you to like me."

"You idiot! Couldn't you tell I *loved* you?"

"How could I? You were engaged to my best friend!" Bill snapped.

"I didn't need to know about the senator for me, Bill. I needed to know about the senator for my parents. I can't help it that all they care about is high society and public image."

Jeff was enjoying seeing someone else in trouble. "Now you want to tell her about the oil wells?"

"No!" Bill returned, glaring at Jeff.

"What oil wells?" Chelsea asked.

"On the family ranch," Jeff said with a smile.

"My dad's in the oil business. He'll be thrilled."

"Yeah, I bet he will be. So, Chelsea, is this your way of telling me that you no longer want to marry me, that you want to pursue a relationship with Bill?" Jeff asked with a smile.

"If you don't mind, Jeff. I think you'd be better off marrying Rebecca since you love her so much. I didn't mean to hurt you or for this to play out the way it has."

"Chelsea, I love you and I thank you. You'll always hold a very special place in my heart, but you're right. I'm in love with Rebecca."

Chelsea took the ring off her third finger. "Here's your ring back."

"Keep it."

"No, she's not keeping another man's ring. Take it back. Maybe you can trade it in," Bill suggested.

Jeff grinned. "Right. I'll see what I can do. Do I need to wait for you before I go see Rebecca?"

"No, I'll take him home in a little while. I think Mom will let me have my car keys after she hears about the oil wells." Chelsea stepped forward and hugged Jeff.

"Hey, no hugging other men," Bill said, teasing.

Chelsea smiled sweetly. "No rules for me, Mr. Wallace." Then she said, "Thank you, Jeff. And I wish you all the happiness in the world."

"I wish you the same, Chelsea. And you've picked a very good man."

"I know," Chelsea agreed, her gaze returning to Bill's face.

Jeff shook Bill's hand and left the room. He found the Wexhams standing in the doorway across the hall.

"Is everything all right?" Mr. Wexham asked.

"Well, Chelsea and I have dissolved our engagement," Jeff said, "but I think Bill is going to take my place."

"Oh, thank heavens," Mrs. Wexham gushed. "Oh, not that I wouldn't have been perfectly happy if she'd married you, Jeff. You know that."

"I know. But Bill is better suited to her, and I need to keep my family together." He waved at them and hurried out the door. He hoped he wasn't too late. If Rebecca ran away and he couldn't find her, he would never forgive her.

Betty answered the door.

"Is Rebecca here?" he asked.

"Yes, sir. She's upstairs. If you'll wait in the library, I'll go tell her you're here."

"Is Will in the library?"

"Yes, sir. And shall I set another plate for dinner?"

"Would you mind, Betty?"

"No, of course not."

"Thanks, Betty."

He'd thought about telling Betty he would go tell Rebecca he was there. He didn't want to give her a chance to run away. But he figured she'd planned to leave in the morning. He remembered how stubborn she'd been about Saturday.

Will was the only one in the library when he got there. "Will, I just invited myself to dinner."

"Good for you. Betty gets depressed if she doesn't have a full house."

"Who's missing besides Rachel?"

"Vanessa went out with some friends. So it was just going to be four of us for dinner. Rebecca, Joey, me and Vivian."

"You know for sure Rebecca intended to be here for dinner?"

Will's gaze fixed on Jeff's face. "What do you mean?"

"I heard a rumor that she was planning on leaving."

"Rebecca? And Joey?"

"Yeah. I think she thought it would be the best thing for my engagement."

"And would it?"

"Yeah, if I wanted the engagement to last."

"But you don't?"

"Not once I knew Rebecca was still single, and I found out about Joey."

"Then why—"

Jeff heard footsteps in the hall and put a finger to his lips. Rebecca entered the library.

"Hello, Jeff. I didn't expect you this evening."

"Well, I was suddenly free and knew Betty wouldn't let me starve. Besides, I didn't get to see much of Joey this week."

"He's with Peter out in the garage. I'll go get him."

"That's not necessary. He'll be in for dinner. Why don't you sit down and visit a little?"

"Okay."

"What did you do with your afternoon off?" Jeff asked.

"Vanessa and I had lunch together. It was fun. We've never really done that before, just the two of us."

Will spoke up. "I think Rachel's leaving this morning was a little hard on all the ladies."

"Why? You know she'll be coming back," Jeff said.

"You never know the twists and turns life will take." Rebecca looked away from Jeff.

"That's true. Where's Vivian?" Jeff asked.

"She's resting upstairs," Will said. "I'd better go see if she's up, though, since Betty will be serving dinner soon."

After Will had left the room, Jeff poked and prodded Rebecca's temper. "Is everything all right, Rebecca?"

"Of course."

"Have you visited with Chelsea recently?"

"You know I just saw her. You specifically asked me to call her and I told you that I went over there."

"Oh, yes. She had a cold, you said. That's the excuse her mother used when she wouldn't call her to the phone."

Rebecca looked at him sharply. "Are you saying her mother was lying?"

Before Jeff answered, Will and Vivian came into the room. They were immediately followed by Betty with a tray of hors d'oeuvres. Then Joey came in because Betty had told him his dad was there.

"Daddy! I haven't seen you since yesterday," he announced as he flung himself into his father's embrace.

Jeff hugged his son tightly to him. "I know, Joey. I missed you a lot."

"Me, too."

"Joey, do you need to go wash up for dinner?" Rebecca asked.

"No, Betty washed my face and hands in the kitchen. And she told Peter it was his fault I got dirty," Joey finished, happy to have it be someone else's fault.

Rebecca looked at her son sternly. "Despite what Betty said, *you* are responsible for getting yourself dirty."

Joey sent a pleading look to his father.

"I'm afraid your mother's right on target this time, son. You have to be responsible for what you do. That's part of growing up."

Betty came in and called them to dinner.

Chapter Sixteen

Rebecca could hardly eat. All she could think about was her promise to Chelsea. She so wished she could take it back. She didn't want to leave these people. Her offer had been on impulse, but she'd known at once it was what was necessary. For herself as well as Chelsea.

She loved Jeff so much. If she stayed here, she would be rooting for him to break up with Chelsea, and that would be a terrible thing to do on her part.

"No appetite?" Jeff asked.

She suddenly realized everyone was staring at her. "I—I had a big lunch with Vanessa. We had the biggest hamburgers...so I have to eat less tonight."

"You sound like Rachel," Vivian said. "I worry about her. I don't think she's eating enough."

"I know. But it's going to take time for Rachel to settle in. She's never known a family like this." Rebecca thought about the fact that she was going to give it up and dropped her gaze to the table. "You'll need to give her time."

Vivian smiled warmly at Rebecca. "With you and

Vanessa to help her, she'll settle soon enough. Right now she's worrying about paying off her debts. She told me she was scheduled almost continuously until Christmas. She was so proud.''

"I don't think modeling is easy work," Rebecca said.

"Neither is being a mother, but you've managed well."

Jeff was smiling at her and she couldn't bear to hold his gaze. He wouldn't be praising her tomorrow. "I try. Sometimes, as a mother, I have to do some unpopular things." She kept a smile on her face and looked at Vivian, hoping she would understand tomorrow.

This departure was the hardest thing she'd ever had to do. Her parting with Jeff five years ago had been involuntary, but this parting was her choice. And it was even more painful.

"Rebecca? Where were you? You seemed to leave us for a minute." Jeff was staring at her again.

"I was thinking about the past, wondering if I made the right decisions."

Will leaned toward her. "Better to leave the past alone. It can't be changed."

"I know." She looked down at Joey and noticed he'd finished his dinner and was beginning to droop with exhaustion. "Joey, are you ready to go up to bed?"

"Yes, Mommy. Can Daddy come, too?"

Jeff responded at once. "I want to. But I've got a phone call I have to make. Then I'll be up."

Rebecca stood, taking Joey's hand, thinking if Jeff knew this would be his last time for a while, he wouldn't linger downstairs too long.

AS SOON AS THE FAMILY HEARD Rebecca and Joey on the stairway, Jeff leaned forward. "I need to take Rebecca out for coffee to meet Bill and Chelsea. They got engaged this afternoon, and I want them to tell Rebecca. She'll believe them when she sees their faces. Then I'm going to propose to Rebecca, which, I hope, will stop her from leaving."

"Leaving?" Vivian questioned, panic rising in her gaze. "Why would she be leaving?"

"It's a long story, but it was because of my engagement to Chelsea. She feels like I've put her and Joey above Chelsea. She's right, of course, but Chelsea and I were always better friends than we were lovers. When I saw how Chelsea responded to Bill, I knew it wouldn't be long before they'd be together. But I couldn't tell Rebecca that."

"Oh, the poor dear. No wonder she was so distracted. When was she planning to leave?" Vivian asked.

"I believe in the morning."

Vivian gasped.

Will said, "Will you give us a call before it gets too late if everything works out? Rebecca has her own key and is certainly too old to have a curfew, but I'd rather Vivian know everything is okay so she can get some sleep."

"Yes, of course. And thank you. I promise I'll take

care of her." He stood. "I've got to call Bill and arrange to meet for coffee, if you'll excuse me."

WHEN THEY LEFT JOEY'S ROOM, Jeff asked Rebecca to go out with him for coffee.

"Why? Betty's coffee is as good as any you can buy."

"Because I want to show you something."

"What?"

"It's a surprise. And once you've seen my surprise, I'll bring you back at once, if that's what you want."

"I don't want to be out late."

"No, of course not."

"I'll have to tell Vivian and Will."

"I've already done that."

"Oh."

"Do you need a jacket?" Jeff asked.

She frowned at him. "No, the air is mild tonight."

"Then let's go."

He took her to the Starbucks near his office. Once there, he bought her a cup of coffee and a pastry.

"I don't need the pastry."

"You hardly ate any dinner. I don't want you passing out on me."

"You're being ridiculous," she said, sounding very grouchy. She had her back to the door, so when Bill and Chelsea came in, she didn't see them until they reached the table, coffee in hand.

"Oh, hi, what are you two doing here?" she asked, staring at their faces. Happiness was written all over the two of them, and Bill kept his arm around Chelsea even after they sat down. Rebecca frowned.

Chelsea laid her left hand on the table. "Can you believe Bill already got me a ring? Isn't it gorgeous?"

Jeff said with a laugh, "That ring must've drained one of the oil wells completely."

"I know. Isn't it divine?" Chelsea asked Rebecca.

Jeff read the shock on Rebecca's face. "I hadn't told her anything. I wanted her to see your happiness for herself. Honey," he said gently, leaning toward Rebecca, "Bill and Chelsea have been falling in love all along. That's why I didn't worry about giving you and Joey all my attention. Today, she finally convinced her parents that he'd be a worthy suitor and broke off her engagement to me."

"Oh, Rebecca, aren't you thrilled everything turned out so well? Now you don't have to leave." Chelsea gave her a relieved smile. "I would've felt so guilty if you'd left for my sake. Now we can really be friends and go shopping together and raise our children together."

"Children?" Rebecca asked, still in shock.

"Well, Bill wants lots of children, but we've come to an agreement on four. We'll have to get started right away. I don't want to be forty and pregnant."

"You'll be the most gorgeous pregnant woman no matter what your age, sweetheart," Bill said.

"As will Rebecca," Jeff said quietly.

"Well, you should know, Jeff. She's already had your first child," Chelsea reminded him with a grin.

"And I missed the whole thing, except for the conception."

Rebecca suddenly stood. "I have to go. I'm very happy for the two of you." Then she headed for the door.

Jeff hurried after her. "I'm sorry I didn't explain things before they got here. I thought you were aware of their attraction to each other, too."

"Please take me back home."

After they got in the car, Jeff asked, "Rebecca, you won't still leave in the morning, will you?"

"No."

"Then can I show you one more thing?"

"What?

"It's another surprise."

"I can't take much more."

He turned into a nearby street, quiet, with stately trees lining it and even statelier homes. When he parked in front of one of them, Rebecca stared at him.

"I can't meet anyone tonight. I'm too—I can't think clearly."

"There's no one in the house. My housekeeper only comes during the day."

"This is your house?" Rebecca asked, her voice rising with signs of hysteria.

He nodded and got out of the car, coming around to open her door. "Come on, honey. I want to show you where I live. It's not a new house, but I've kept it in good condition, and I really like it."

She followed him up the curving sidewalk to the

front door. He pulled out a key and opened the door. Then he turned and invited her in.

She stepped into the house, immediately loving it. It could use a little more color in its decor, but it had wonderful possibilities.

"It's lovely, Jeff. Now I really have to go."

"Not yet, Rebecca." His voice was firm.

"But you promised—"

"I know I did. But tonight is our first time together when I'm free from any entanglements, and I can do what I've wanted to do since that first day I saw you at my office." He suddenly dropped to one knee and took her hand in his.

She stared at him.

He didn't waste any time. "Rebecca Barlow, will you marry me? Will you and Joey come live with me and be a family? Nothing in this world would make me happier."

Instead of a joyful acceptance of his offer, Rebecca burst into tears.

He stood and took her in his arms. "Rebecca, what's wrong?"

"I don't want you to be forced into marriage. I promise I won't leave. I'll let you see Joey as often as you want. I'll—"

He kissed her, one of those deep, soulful kisses that always turns a woman inside out.

When he finally raised his lips from hers, he whispered, "But I want to make more Joeys, or Josettes or whatever the feminine form is. I want to share my life with you until we're both too old to remember all the joyous years we've had together. I want to be surrounded by our grandchildren and great-grand-children. Most of all, I want you, Rebecca, and no one else.'' He looked into her eyes. ''I can't tell you I've been celibate for five years, but there were only a couple of ladies, and I never repeated it. Because every time, I realized it was nothing like making love to you. I never made love to Chelsea because we were friends, not lovers.''

He kissed her again and her arms went around his neck and she held on for dear life. When he whispered in her ear, ''Please say yes,'' she barely had the breath to answer, but he heard the definite yes.

''Oh, Becca, I've been waiting for this day ever since I saw you in English class back in school. I just never thought it would take so long.''

''Me, neither.''

He kissed her several more times, their bodies heating as they shared themselves. When he buried his face in her hair, she said, ''Where's the bedroom?''

He stiffened. ''I should take you home.''

She took a step back. ''I'm too forward for you? Have you changed your mind?''

''Never. But I promised myself I wouldn't make love to you until my wedding ring was on your finger,'' he explained.

''Do you think I trust you any less now than I did five years ago when I gave you my virginity? I didn't do so because I loved sex. I did so because I loved you. And I still do.''

He pulled her into his arms, holding her tightly. "I don't deserve you."

"Yes, you do. And the time will come when you think you got taken, so just remember you said that."

"That time will never happen."

"You haven't seen me in labor yet," she assured him with a chuckle.

"Oh, how I wish I had. I regret what happened so much."

"As Will said, the past can't be changed. The future can. Should I ask again, where's the bedroom?"

"Are you sure?"

"More sure than anything I've done in the past five years."

He took her hand and started up the stairs. "At least this will be a first for us."

"Oh?"

"Yeah, in a bed. We always made love in the back seat of my car."

"I know. And it wasn't as nice as the car you have now, but it was bigger. Our daughters are going to be warned about smooth talkers with a big back seat."

"Our daughters aren't going to be allowed out of the house until they're thirty."

"Famous last words. You think Joey's got you wrapped around his little finger? Wait until a little girl with curls and big blue eyes begs for something."

"I'll tell her to ask her mother." He opened the door to a large room. To Rebecca, the most important furniture at that moment was the big king-size bed. She started toward it.

"Wait a minute," Jeff said.

"You're having second thoughts?"

"No. I promised Will I'd call and tell them you weren't leaving before they went to bed."

"You told them I was leaving?"

"Yeah, I think that came out." He looked guilty, but he moved to the phone beside the bed and dialed the number. "Will, it's Jeff. Rebecca isn't leaving after all. She's going to marry me." He paused and then said, "As soon as possible."

Rebecca had followed him across the room. She lifted the phone from his hand. "Will, I won't be home until morning. May we join you for breakfast?" After a pause, she said, "Thank you, goodbye."

"Did you have to tell him that?"

"Did you have to tell him I was leaving?"

"I would've told the world if it stopped you from walking out of my life a second time. I barely survived the first time."

"Me, too," she whispered, walking into his embrace again. "I have so longed to be one with you. I'm hungry for your arms to hold me."

"I never want you to be hungry again, my love."

Their first mating went quickly, wildly, satisfying the aches that had been waiting for five years.

The second time, several hours later, was a savoring, a remembrance of their few times together. Each time Jeff used a condom, though he told Rebecca he intended to work on those brothers and sisters for Joey as soon as they were married.

"How many children do you want?" Rebecca asked as she stroked his chest.

"Four sounds like a good number to me. How many do you want?"

"Well, I suppose we should keep up with the Wallaces, you know. Or we could have five just to be sure they know we're overachievers."

"We're going to get an early start. They're planning on waiting for June to marry. I have next weekend in mind. How does that sound to you?"

"As long as Rachel is back by then. She and Vanessa and Will and Vivian and Betty and Peter need to be there. And Joey, of course."

"We'll need to have Bill and Chelsea there, too, I think. And Harriet, of course. They're the only family I have." He kissed her neck.

She brought his mouth to hers, a joining of passion that had driven their lovemaking.

"If we keep doing this, I'm going to have to get dressed and go out."

Rebecca sat up, clutching the sheet to her bare breasts. "Why? Where would you go?"

"To an all-night store to buy some more condoms. I only have one left and I'm saving it for in the morning."

"Why in the morning and not now?"

"Because it's long been a fantasy of mine to wake up in bed with you and make love as the sun rises," he whispered before he kissed her again.

"Then start getting dressed. I want you to have your fantasy."

"But I have one left. I don't— Oh. I'll be right back," he said, and grabbed his jeans.

"I hope so," she said sweetly. "Just don't have any wrecks. I'm not going anywhere."

He gave her a big smile. "I know, and nothing could make me happier than that."

Epilogue

The chapel on the Southern Methodist University campus was available only for a noon wedding. So two weeks later, at noon, Jeff and Rebecca became husband and wife in front of all their family, real or adopted.

Afterward, they returned to Vivian and Will's house, where Betty had prepared a sumptuous feast and a beautiful wedding cake that even Chelsea admired.

Joey, dressed in a new suit his father had bought him, had listened to all their explanations about what would happen and why, but he still seemed rather confused.

"Mommy, why can't we still live here with Grandpa Will and Grandma Vivian?"

"Because when people get married, they live together, sweetie. You have a nice bedroom at Daddy's house, don't you?"

"Yes, but I want to keep my bedroom here."

"Joey, that's not—"

Vivian interrupted. "How about we keep it just the

way it is so when you come visit, you'll feel at home?''

"I'd like that. Can I come visit often?''

"Anytime you want, dear.''

"Daddy, Grandma Vivian said I can come visit anytime I want.''

"That's nice of her. By the way, I thought you should have a gift, too, on our wedding day. Would you like to have it now?''

Dinner was complete and the wedding cake served, and presents opened. It seemed as if everyone was waiting for something.

Rebecca guessed it was Jeff's gift to Joey. He must've told everyone but her. He would have to get over this surprise fetish he had.

She didn't realize Bill had left the room until he returned. In his arms, he carried a golden retriever puppy. The little dog was trembling with nervousness.

"A puppy? I can have a puppy?''

"Yes. I thought you'd like to have him to sleep with you.''

"He can sleep in my bed? Did you ask Mommy?'' Joey had his eyes on Rebecca, not sure she'd agree to such a thing.

Jeff stood and put his arms around Rebecca. "What do you say, Mom? Can Joey have his puppy?''

"I suppose so, but I don't think he should sleep with him until he's trained.''

"He's already been trained. All we have to do is train Joey.'' Everyone laughed at that.

"What are you going to name your puppy, Joey?" Rebecca asked.

"I don't know. He's kind of like my baby brother, isn't he? Grandma Vivian, what are you going to name your baby?"

"We don't know yet, Joey. We don't know if it's a girl or a boy."

"Oh. Well, I think I'll name him…" He studied the puppy. The little dog, now in Joey's arms, reached up and licked his face.

"He likes you, Joey," Rebecca said, "and he's a little boy, too."

"I think I'll name him Davy. That's the little boy in my favorite book. Is that okay?"

"That's fine. You and Davy will be very happy. Did you thank your father?"

"Aw, Mom, we're married now. He's supposed to give me presents."

"Joey Jacobs, manners are important, married or not."

"Thank you, Daddy, for Davy. I love him."

"I'm glad, son."

Joey wasn't through. "And thank you, Mommy, for finding Daddy. He's the bestest present ever."

Will knelt down and put an arm around Joey. "Well said, Joey. Family is the best present anyone can ever receive."

Everyone toasted their glasses, joining in with Joey's feelings.

Rebecca looked at her husband. In a whisper, she said, "Thank you for giving me Joey."

"I'm the lucky one. You took care of our son until I could help. Most men aren't that lucky. Now we're a family and no one will ever tear us apart." Then he kissed her.

Joey looked at all the guests. "They do that all the time."

Everyone laughed again, Vanessa and Rachel sharing a smile. They were sad that Rebecca would be moving out of the house, but she would be close by, and her happiness was obvious to everyone.

After the kiss, Jeff turned to their guests. "We want to thank you for being with us today and sharing our happiness. One more toast, to family. I now have one, and I hope it keeps growing."

Will sighed, "I'm doing my best."

Vivian patted her stomach. "You certainly are."

Everyone roared with laughter as Will tried to explain he meant finding David, the other brother, and convincing Jim to come home from the Middle East.

"However we get them, Will, we'll take them. And if you run out of bedrooms here, I have a few to spare at my house," Jeff added.

With that, he picked up Joey and his puppy and put an arm around Rebecca. "We're going home. Come visit whenever you're in the neighborhood."

They were a real family at last.

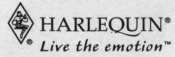

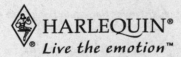

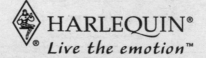

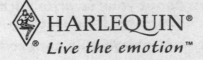

If you enjoyed what you just read,
then we've got an offer you can't resist!

Take 2 bestselling
love stories FREE!
Plus get a FREE surprise gift!